Martha,

Happy reading!

Sloan St. James

The Dark Shield

The Dark Shield
Sloan St.James

Tiger Publications

Lemont, Illinois
www.tigerpublications.com

Dedication

To my granddaughter, Marissa, who's branded my heart with her love.

Acknowledgements

I would like to thank the Director of the Society of Druidism for his help through the quagmire of the ancient rituals.

Once more I would like to thank Chrys Wagner for waving her magic wand over my words and bringing out the best in them.

Lastly, I would like to thank my family for all their love and support through these many years.

Prologue

August 15, 1998

SHE WAS DEAD!

With trembling fingers, he brushed back the strand of blonde hair that had fallen across her forehead. He'd learned too late that her love was his heart's destiny. Now death had stolen the softness of her voice, the gentleness of her touch, and extinguished the blue fire in her eyes. He drew in a slow breath. The air in his lungs congealed as he ran his knuckles down the line of her jaw. She had vanquished the emptiness in his heart, and he repaid her with death. The memory of her in his arms ripped open his heart, and he buried his anguish-filled tears in her chest. The primordial law dictated an eye for an eye, a soul for a soul. Would he have the strength to face what **had** to be done? He lifted his eyes to the starless sky and his heart whispered, "yes."

Chapter 1

June 7, 1998

Inside the old brick building, naked light bulbs dangled from their cords like hanged men, while shadows shifted over the green-scarred walls. Outside, the muffled sounds of Chicago waking up camouflaged the soft creaking footsteps on the old wooden stairs.

A rivulet of sweat ran down Conner Wolfe's spine. Yesterday's early summer heat and humidity, held captive in the narrow hallway, made the air reek of garbage and urine. The stench of decaying futures had Conner straining a breath through his teeth. He swallowed hard to push down the bile and memories that assaulted him.

Instinctively, Conner's fingers tightened around the gun in his hand. He tried to remember how easily it was to be drawn into the false sense of security that the cold steel offered. A cop only put his trust in his gut and his partner. That's how you got out alive.

An infant's scream sent the four police officers flat against the wall. Their wide eyes slashed in every direction at once. Adrenaline amplified even the most miniscule sound. Yet, in the silent spaces between the thundering beats of his heart, Conner heard only one thing: the sound of fear.

He snapped his gaze over the ridge of his shoulder to his partner. When Gene Bonkowski nodded his gray head, Conner released his pent up breath. He knew the veteran cop would never give the okay if a bust had the slightest chance of going south.

Conner motioned with the barrel of his gun for the others to follow. Then, just as he raised his foot to take the next step, a hail of angry shouts and bullets ricocheted down into the stairwell. Conner dove to the floor. Using the stairs as a shield, he repeatedly fired off rounds at the two dark figures that sprayed the stairwell with bullets.

"Keep your heads down!" Conner shouted.

Before he could take his next breath, a flash of light exploded against the right side of his face. Suddenly, he was fighting against the draw of a spiraling vortex that sucked him deeper and deeper into its black core. Then, as quickly as it had begun, the spinning stopped.

"What's happened?! Gene?! Ray!? Jake!? What the hell is going on?"

Out of the darkness, tiny lights shimmered, moving and shifting until they formed the gilded points of a face. Conner's heart hammered in his chest. While every muscle in his body quaked, he stared at the image. Then, with all the air in his lungs, Conner hurled out the name he'd kept buried for so long.

"PETER!"

Warm tears ran down Conner's face as the blood in his veins chilled. Memories flashed through his mind. Each picture was vivid and clear but quickly dissolved like melting film. As the scenes disappeared, grief scaled Conner's heart. "Peter," Conner said on an indrawn breath.

"Don't be cryin', Niall," the raspy voice whispered past Conner's ear.

Quickly, Conner choked back his tears. "Oh Peter, I'll not be cryin', I promise," Conner answered through a tear-clogged throat. "Please Peter, don't be a dyin'. I promise I'll nay be a cryin'. Don't be leavin' me alone, please."

Fear and loneliness racked Conner's body. As his trembling hand reached out for the fading image, he shivered with a cold that reached deep into his soul. For twenty years he'd kept the secret, and now that unforgiven sin screamed out for retribution. Conner sucked in a ragged breath. What would his penance be for murdering ten-year-old Niall Malone?

A crashing pain exploded in Conner's head and hurled him out of the arms of the blue-gray fog. He tried to claw the pain out through his eye sockets, but something thick covered them.

"Goddammit." The word scratched through his dry throat while fragmented scenes flashed behind his closed eyes. One after another, they flipped forward.

4

He'd been shot!

Conner tore at the bandages, but the weight of a hand pressing on his shoulder stopped him. "Please, Mr. Wolfe, you mustn't do that." The soft feminine voice didn't match the strength of the fingers that anchored him to the bed.

"My partner and the others, are they ok? I have to know."

"I don't know, Mr. Wolfe. Please, just relax."

Conner sucked in a breath and tossed out his next question. "Am I blind? Do I have any face left?" He'd squeezed his questions so tightly together there wasn't a breath between them.

"Just relax, Mr. Wolfe. Your doctor will be in shortly," the soft voice answered in sterile and controlled tones.

"Please," Conner begged through a heavy whisper, "please, just tell me?"

"Relax," she stated flatly.

Anger shoved away what little tolerance he had left, and Conner pushed himself upright. "Relax? How in the hell can I do that when I don't even know where I am?"

After a moment, she answered, "You're in St. Phelim's Hospital."

Before Conner could jerk out of her grasp, her fingers dug into his forearm and a needle pierced his skin. The instant that the hot liquid flooded his veins, he took a deep breath. The amalgamated aromas of soft perfume and harsh disinfectant filled his lungs and swirled in his brain.

"You didn't have to pump that shit into me. I'll behave."

"We have to ensure we won't need to tie you to the bed again."

"Again?" Conner questioned over a thickening tongue.

The sedative snaked through him, pulling him into the dark pit of nothingness. Conner fought hard against the siphon, but it was no use. The abyss devoured him in an overwhelming sense of desolation. At that instant he knew that once more he'd been the lone survivor.

A tear slipped out the corner of his eye. "Alone." His mind repeated the word like a mantra. "Alone. Alone." Then, out of the darkness, a small blue flower floated toward him, its petals as delicate as the small hand that held it. When the flower fell into Conner's hand, the darkness around him lightened, and the face of a blonde-haired child smiled at him. Flames danced in her blue eyes, and the loneliness that had gripped his heart melted away. He sighed. He wasn't alone. She was there.

"When the bandages come off, I want you to keep your eyes

closed until I tell you to open them," the doctor instructed as he slowly picked at the tape holding the patches that covered Conner's eyes.

"Sure," Conner shot out on an exhale.

The correlation between Dr. Edward Kresner's slow words and the speed at which he removed each layer of tape and gauze was obvious. Anxiety pricked Conner's nerves. To keep from knocking the doctor's hand aside and ripping the bandages off himself, Conner tightened his grip on the metal arms of the chair.

Since learning that two of the cops had been killed in that stairwell and that his partner, Gene, had died hours later at the hospital, Conner wavered through depression, guilt, and anger. He hated being left behind. Now, at this moment, he added anxiety to the list. It had been four days since the shooting, and the moment of reckoning had arrived. He was about to learn his own fate. When the last piece of tape tugged at his skin, tension flipped Conner's stomach. He drew in a slow breath. A cool breeze wafted over his closed eyes, and it took every ounce of his reserve to keep from opening his eyes.

"Hmmmmmm." The doctor's tone didn't help temper Conner's mounting anxiety. "The angle the bullet took was a pretty clear path," Dr. Kresner said, touching his fingers to the tender spot above his patient's right eyebrow.

Conner bit his lip.

"Are you having pain?" the doctor asked quickly.

"Sorta." Conner mixed the word through a nervous chuckle. "The tension is killin' me, Doc."

"Okay," the doctor said while sliding a pair of glasses onto Conner's face. "Nance, would you turn off the lights, please?"

The deep tone of the doctor's voice lowered then rose again as he said, "Now, open your eyes slowly. Slowly." The doctor's repeated instruction fanned Conner's face.

Conner tried lifting his eyelids, but they wouldn't budge. For a split second, he'd thought they'd been sewn shut. Then on his second try, they opened. At first, Conner could see only blackness, but when the doctor slipped off the glasses, the color shifted to a murky gray. Silvery lines swam inside the swarthy blur. Slowly, the ebony silhouettes congealed, and Conner chuckled, "I see something. It's not clear, but I can see."

"That's good. Yes, blurred is good," Kresner said. Simultaneously he touched each corner of Conner's eyes. "That'll all clear up, but for now, I want you to get used to the dim light.

6

After a few minutes we'll turn them up."

The doctor's finger grazed over a tender spot on Conner's forehead again, but this time he saw the shadow coming.

"Let's give it just a minute more," the doctor repeated.

A minute!? Conner wanted to bark out. What good would a minute do? But instead, he answered with a small, "uh huh."

After the full minute passed, the doctor replaced the sunglasses on Conner's face and stood up. "You can turn up the lights now, Nancy."

Even behind the black lenses, the rush of light sent a white-hot pain exploding inside Conner's head. "Holy shit." He sucked the words through his teeth, and slammed his eyes shut. When the horrendous pain that hammered against his skull leveled out, Conner lifted his head. He blinked a few times and the out-of-focus images took on more definition.

"Damn! I really can see."

The doctor slowly slid the glasses off again. Conner sucked in a breath while he waited for the pain. This time only small pricks attacked his eyes, and Conner released his pent up breath.

As the doctor's features sharpened, Conner smiled. Dr. Kresner wasn't the ol' country doc type Conner had imagined. Instead, the man was as bald as a cue ball and had a face that should've been in a wrestling ring. Conner wanted to laugh out loud, but then his thoughts jumped to the nurse. Would the image created by her delicate touch and subtle perfume match the one he'd conjured up in his mined? Conner turned in his chair and was hit by the shocked, wide-eyed look on the gray-haired woman's face. It was all the answer Conner needed. He snapped his gaze around and grabbed for the mirror that sat on the table in front of him.

He sucked in a ragged breath and held it while he stared at his reflection. The image that looked back at him had his same sandy colored hair, same square jaw line, and the same blue eyes. Conner shifted his head to the left. Above his right eyebrow was a single red dot the size of a nickel where the bullet had entered. Conner touched it lightly then turned his head to the right and took in the full force of what the bullet had done to his face.

A brownish-purple ring encircled each eye and spread down his swollen cheeks. A sutured gash ran a jagged path from his eye socket to the corner of his mouth. From each stitch, tiny dots of blood-tainted fluid wept.

Conner strangled the mirror's handle with his fingers, then slowly turned it over and placed it back on the table. The weight of what he'd seen pulled his chin to his chest. He closed his eyes and balled his fists. Who was the nameless person who looked back at him? Suddenly, he knew. It was the arrogant face of a selfish parasite.

Chapter 2

"I'm sure, after a week of being fed hospital food, you're looking forward to something that doesn't taste like wallpaper paste," Jack Wolfe stated while squeezing the last of his son's flower arrangements onto a metal cart. "Mom and Father Tim have been cooking since daybreak. I'm sure there'll be enough food to feed a small country by dinner time."

With his gaze lowered, Conner tossed his rolled up clothes into the black zippered bag. His dad's small talk wasn't making the transition from the cloistered world of the hospital to the cavernous one outside any easier. In fact, Jack's idle conversation was quickly grating on Conner's nerves. Then again, since the bandages had come off, everything grated on his nerves.

"Looks like our favorite patient is checking out," announced the redheaded nurse as she entered the room.

Without lifting his gaze, Conner nodded.

"Yep, his mother is anxious to take over where you 'Florence Nightingales' left off," Jack said, filling in Conner's silent reply.

"Well, I've got a list of instructions from your doctor and a whole bunch of papers that need your signature, but first, I have to give your bracelet a quick check." The nurse giggled and stepped to Conner's side. "Gotta make sure you're the real Conner Wolfe."

Conner stabbed his father's face with wide eyes.

Jack winked at his son, but he spoke to the nurse. "Wouldn't do for the wrong Conner breakin' outta here, huh?"

Reluctantly extending his hand to the nurse, Conner continued to search his father's face, the same way he'd done that morning twenty years ago at Shannon airport.

"It'd be much worse," the nurse tittered, while taking hold of Conner's hand, "if we sent the wrong one the bill."

When she pulled the band of plastic taunt against Conner's wrist, he felt his heart quicken. He cornered his eyes to see if she noticed the change in his pulse. Before he could gauge the lines in her face, Jack draped his arm over Conner's shoulder. The warmth of it rushed through him.

Time had tipped Jack Wolfe's dark sideburns silver and added scored lines to his brow. He still cut an imposing figure that did his six foot four frame proud. Yet, though fifty wasn't old, there was no mistaking an old soul's reflection in his whiskey colored eyes. Conner smiled up at Jack. There was a strength in those dark centers that Conner learned early on he could always trust. That trust was at the core of their family. To Jack, his family was his purpose, his destiny.

His thoughts pulled the corners of Conner's smile down. He believed being a cop was his destiny, but the bullet changed that when it caused limited vision in his eye. Conner's face warmed with the heat of anger. Once again, a bullet changed the course of his life's path.

The nurse handed Conner a single sheet of paper and drew a finger over a line at the bottom of the page. "You need to sign here. Then we'll have you on your way."

Conner's hand shook when he reached for the pen.

"Here, son." Jack removed the paper from under Conner's shaking hand. "Let me make sure you're not signing away the family farm."

Conner watched Jack scan the form. It was obvious his father still took his protective role seriously. Today, Jack was saving his son from embarrassment in front of a pretty nurse. Twenty years ago, it was Conner's life.

"Gosh, the wheelchair is here already," the nurse said as an orderly maneuvered the chair into the room.

After tucking his bag under his arm, Conner folded into the chair. "Dad, are you finished with those papers?" Conner asked, looking up at Jack.

"Oh yeah, sure, son," Jack answered with a feigned surprised look on his face. He pushed the paper onto the bag resting on Conner's lap.

Jack winked at the nurse and said, "You better put your John Hancock on the dotted line or this pretty little thing won't let me take you home."

With a shaking hand, Conner scribbled his name across the line and handed the paper to the nurse. "Sorry, the signature isn't good. The bag's not easy to write on."

She carried her wide smile from Jack to the paper. "No problem. As long as you're the real Conner Wolfe."

Conner drew the bag tighter to his chest. He clenched his teeth to keep the words in his mind from leaping out his mouth, but that didn't stop his mind from screaming, "I'm not the real Conner Wolfe. Conner Wolfe is dead."

Between the small patches of conversation, Conner lobbed his head back against the car seat and closed his eyes. A soft sigh slipped through his lips while summer sunlight warmed his face. The warmth felt good on his skin, but guilt chilled his heart. Three good men had been killed. That was the second time fate stepped in and forced him to survive when others around him had died. What kind of cruel joke was life always playing on him?

"You okay, son?"

"Sure," Conner answered from behind closed eyes.

Mixed with a gush of air, Jack replied, "Good."

A strange feeling crept up Conner's spine. He opened his eyes and turned to his father. Jack's attention was centered on the traffic, but the normally straight line of his shoulders had curved downward.

"Are you okay, Dad?"

Jack flashed a quick smile and nodded to the windshield. "But, I think you should know that Mom and Father Tim have planned a little homecoming celebration."

Conner quickly pushed himself up in the seat. Holding his father's profile in his sight, Conner narrowed his eyes. "What kind of celebration?"

After a cluck of his tongue, Jack answered, "You know how Tim gets; 'little' means he's put a notice in the church bulletin and probably one in every parish or synagogue within a fifteen mile radius."

"Jesus Christ, Dad, I don't want people to see me like this!"

"Son, you don't look as bad as you think."

"As bad as what? Frankenstein? Quasimodo?" Conner lashed out. He pulled his shoulders up to hide between them.

Jack shot his son a quick glance, then put his attention back to the traffic. "Trust me. You're exaggerating."

Conner turned fully in the seat and whipped off his sunglasses.

"You think this is an exaggeration?"

Though Jack didn't turn in response to his son's demand to look at him, Conner still held his father's profile in a hard narrow-eyed glare.

After a full second, Jack's words came out like a warmed blanket. "You keep watching me like that and all you'll ever see is love in my eyes."

With a sharp huff through his nose, Conner snapped his gaze back to the windshield. His actions didn't stop Jack from going down the verbal path he'd started. "I don't care if you have six eyes and no nose. You're my son. I love you unconditionally, and that scar on your face doesn't take one bit away from the wonderful person inside you."

Glaring at the near space beyond the windshield, Conner pulled his chin to his chest and hissed out over his curled lips. "I don't know who that person is."

Conner didn't have to look at his father to know how he'd react. However, if Conner had any doubts, they were quickly erased with the surprised tone of Jack's voice. "Oh, so then just who do you think you are?"

Slamming his sunglasses back over his eyes, Conner tossed his answer out. "I don't have a goddamn clue."

"Cala, wouldya stop fussing in the kitchen, already. They'll be here any minute," the priest called out, refusing to turn his attention away from the window.

Outside, a quick breeze shook the branches of the large oak trees lining the street, and speckles of sunshine danced across the black pavement. Father Tim Sladek smiled. He remembered the day those trees were planted and the burly man barking orders at the crew that dug the holes.

James Wolfe was a huge man, but the way he lovingly placed each tree into the hole was like a father tucking his child into bed. Tim didn't know it then, but Jack's father felt more than mere professional pride for those trees. The Wolfes had just bought a house on this same street and their son was just about Tim's age.

The priest winced with the stinging memory of the role he played in welcoming the scrawny Wolfe kid to the neighborhood. Under Tim's direct leadership, the "gang" tormented Jack with jaunts and jeers every time he met up with them.

Then, one Saturday afternoon, while riding his bike through the park, Tim came upon Jack and his father. The pair was crouched down to the ground studying something in the grass. Tim stopped a few feet away to watch.

"Hey there lad, would ya like to be seein' some baby rabbits?" James called out. Tim walked his bike over, but pulled up short of the pair. The older Wolfe motioned to Tim. "Come here now, they'll nay be bitin' ya."

Tim moved in and lowered down next to Jack's side. James lifted the patch of dried grass, and the two boys peered into the burrow together. They looked at the baby rabbits and then at each other. Jack smiled at Tim, and Tim returned the smile. At that moment, their friendship was born.

Running a grazing finger over the dark wood of the windowsill, Tim sighed. That same day he'd been invited in to share cookies and milk. Over forty years later they were still sharing food and friendship in the same house.

"You're knowin' the lad doesn't like green peppers, and you've put a ton of them in the salad," Cala Wolfe reprimanded as she entered the room.

The sound of her voice jolted Tim completely around. "Conner can just pick them out like he always does," Tim answered through a smile.

Wiping her hands on the towel she'd carried into the room, Cala shook her head, fanning out the dark ends of her short-cropped hair. "Och, but today 'tis his day. So the salad should be to his likin', not yours."

After a hard tsk through his teeth, Tim returned his gaze to the scene out the window. "The boy has eaten nothing but hospital food this last week. I'm sure he'll eat anything that's not moving, even if it is a green pepper."

Cala stepped to the priest's side to share the view. "More's the reason to be spoilin' him."

Tim couldn't hold back an exploding laugh, but through it he said, "I think that table in there can vouch for the spoiling part." He cocked his head and hitched his thumb in the direction of the dining room to put an exclamation point to his statement.

The table was dressed with Cala's best Irish lace cloth. Light glinted off creamy white china plates and sparkled through the long stemmed crystal glasses. Every inch of the table was taken up by an array of steaming dishes. Slightly askew on the wall behind the table hung a white banner with large, irregular black letters that read, "Welcome Home Conner." Cala's mark of love was everywhere in this old house, but no place more than in the hearts of her husband and son.

Tim held his smile in check. "You've had me up since the break of dawn chopping, slicing, polishing, and Lord knows what all else, and you'd begrudge me a few slices of green peppers for my trouble?"

Cala slammed her hands on her hips and speared the priest with her piercing blue eyes. "Father Timothy Sladek, 'twas yourself that came a bangin' on our door well before the cock crowed. You was a totin' bags of fixin's and shoutin' that there's things need doin' for the lad's homecomin'." Cala's finger came up in a sharp point, and she waggled it directly under the priest's nose while she finished her artificial tirade. "'Tis yourself that's the culprit, Bucko."

In a futile attempt to keep it under control, Tim covered his smile with his hand. Her brogue became prominent when she wanted it to. She was a true Irish lass, born in Tirnageata, Ireland. It was there she and Jack had met.

The priest looked down at Cala's upturned face and caught the glinting smile in her eyes. Pushing the corners of his mouth down, Tim diverted his gaze to keep the effect. "I knew you'd be at my door the minute the sun came up, so I wanted to beat you to the punch."

"Punch, my foot! You've been missin' the boy just as much as Jack and myself." Cala stepped to Tim's side and tugged his hand from his mouth. Tenderness swam in her eyes. "Thank you for holdin' our boy close to your heart and petitionin' Our Lord to be leavin' the lad with us a bit longer."

While a knot squeezed his heart, Tim gently covered her hand with his. "There's no need to thank me. I'm just grateful all our prayers were answered."

Cala returned his smile, then turned back to the window and spoke softly into the glass. "We're blessed, 'tis true. I thank the Almighty that Jack didn't have to lose another son."

"I think that's a lesson neither of you needed to learn again in this lifetime."

Before Tim could finish his thought, Cala pushed away from the window. "There's Jack's car now," she shouted, rounding the priest.

Tim slammed his hand over his ear and rubbed the sting out of it. "Damn, woman, I need that ear to hear confessions."

Cala carried her laughter out the door.

Chapter 3

"*Baile failte*! *Baile failte, Ahmac*," Cala cried tearfully while running down the flight of stairs.

Conner had just pulled himself out of the car when she enveloped him in her arms.

"Welcome home," she whispered in his ear. She tightened her embrace and brushed a kiss to his cheek. "Welcome home, son."

Unshed tears clogged in Conner's throat while her warmth rippled through him. He encircled her in his arms and drew in the soft floral scent that clung to her hair. "Thanks, Mom." His words came out in just above a whisper after being strained through strangled emotions.

Cala looked up into his face and released a ragged sigh. The smile in her eyes spread to her mouth, and she tenderly brushed back a wisp of hair from his forehead. "You're still quite a dashin' lad, you know. The scar will only be addin' a bit of character to your good looks."

"Sure, it will. Character enough to make Halloween masks." Conner immediately regretted what he'd said. He never wanted to hurt the woman who had given him life. How could he be so insensitive to slap her with his anger? Conner released the tension in his jaw and forced a small smile. Cala opened their embrace. With one arm circled around his waist, she led him up the stairs.

Inside the open doorway, Tim stood with a smile as bright as the white collar he wore around his neck. His hand shot out to Conner. "Just so you don't go thinking this is an important day, or anything, I made the salad and loaded it with green peppers."

Before Conner could accept the priest's hand, he found himself pulled into a bone-crushing hug that pushed the air out of his

15

lungs in a gush.

"Nice to see you too, Father Tim."

Conner's so-called homecoming wasn't much more than a few of his close friends stopping by sporadically throughout the evening. They were all generous with their well wishes, but stingy with talk about the shooting, everyone, that is, except Gene Bonkowski's daughter, Angela.

When Angela arrived, Cala led the young woman into the living room and gestured for her to have a seat in the chair directly across from Conner. He had a difficult time lifting his gaze to Angela's face. How could he look into her eyes after he'd gotten her father killed? Conner drew in a deep breath for strength and forced his gaze to her face.

"Would you be likin' something to drink, Miss Bonkowski?" Cala asked, taking a step in the direction of the kitchen.

The blue-eyed, brunette, woman, just out of her teens, smiled easily. "Please, call me Angie."

"Well, then Angie," Cala said with a small smile and nod. "May I get you some refreshments?"

Angie's smile widened with her reply. "No, thank you, Mrs. Wolfe."

With her refusal, Angie's smile quickly washed away, and her gaze moved to Conner's face. "I won't stay long. I've only come to give you this," she said, pulling a small box from the pocket of her jean jacket. Her gaze lowered with her voice. "It's from my father."

"What?" The one-word question only partially came out around the lump in Conner's throat.

The young woman leaned forward, with the box cradled in her two hands. "Dad left this for you."

Conner braced his elbows on his knees and folded his hands together. He threaded and unthreaded his fingers repeatedly while he kept his gaze locked on Angie's round face. Conner didn't try to say anything. He knew it would never come out.

Cala immediately chimed in. "Oh my dear, you're so kind."

Turning to Cala, Angie answered, "But this isn't from me, Ma'am."

"Yes, you said that," Cala nodded her answer, "Yet 'tis your kindness that brought the gift to our son."

Angie lowered her head and took a small breath. Her thumbs gently stroked the edged of the package. "Dad was a good cop." She pulled her spine straight, as if she needed strength to step away from the painful thought. When she brought her head up, her eyes met Conner's. The sheen of unshed tears confirmed her emotions were very near the surface. She softly cleared her throat. "Dad said you were a good cop, too."

Conner hadn't realized he'd reached for the box until he felt the weight of it in his hands.

"In the hospital, before Dad died, he'd asked me to give that to you. I was to tell you he was sorry for making the mistake that got you shot."

"No, I made the mistake, not your father," Conner fired his words out.

With a small shake of her head, Angie negated Conner's statement long before his words settled down. "Even though it was your bust, Dad knew he was the one calling the shots that morning. This was his way to try to correct his mistake."

Conner lifted the lid of the small box. Inside, nestled in a bed of dark blue velvet, was Chicago police shield number 3964, Gene Bonkowski's badge.

A small glint sparked off the polished metal. Conner's hand trembled. It matched the vibrating beats of his heart. A dark shadow fell over the shield, and suddenly the shimmer died. It died just like Gene had died, just like Peter had died. Who would be next to be sacrificed for this fallacious entity the world has been tricked into believing was Conner Wolfe?

Gray clouds churned and twisted over the horizon, closing up the gaping holes in the blue sky. Conner sat on the highest level of concrete blocks that outlined the lake's shore. Lake Michigan was angry. This inland water had the reputation of being even more dangerous than the ocean when it had a mind to, and today looked to be one of those days. Each wave that rushed to shore slapped against the retaining wall and sent an enraged arm of water high into the air. The torrent spray darkened the soft gray boulders to match the menacing clouds rolling in the sky.

Just offshore, masts of moored sailboats rocked back and forth with each gust of wind. Along the lake's edge, runners who dotted the path weren't the least bit interested in the monster that sat on the shore. Conner curled his lip and huffed. That's how he thought of himself, a monster that feeds off others so it would live.

In the two weeks since he'd been released from the hospital, the scar had faded into nothing more than a jagged red line. Though the wound on his cheek had healed, he felt the wounds from his past festering. He tried to make sense of it all, but nothing fit. Why had his life been spared? His wasn't more valuable than the others.

Father Tim always preached that God makes no mistakes, that everything happens for a reason, and that it's our responsibility to find out the purpose He has for us, the "almighty plan" theory. Conner moved his head slightly from side to side. There was no way he could be so egotistical as to think God's plan for him was so important that lives were sacrificed for his sake. If Conner didn't believe in God, then he could easily be swayed to believe that human evolution was nothing more than pond scum gone awry.

He blew out a hard tsk with his frustration. Divine plan or not, no one individual should take precedence over another. In God's eyes, we're all equal.

A deep rumbling growl vibrated in Conner's throat while he struggled through the quagmire of why things were like they were. He needed to know where his life was going. A cop searched for clues to solve a mystery, but Conner didn't have enough to go on, not here, anyway. All he knew was that his life had changed in Belfast the day his biological father walked out.

The wind brushed past Conner ear and swept down his collar. Conner pulled in his chin and tucked his head deeper into his shirt. When a chill crawled up his spine, Conner strained a breath through his teeth. An aroma of baked potatoes brought a rush of painful memories. He turned away from the lake and shook off the unpleasant memories with the half-hearted explanation that the smell came from the restaurants along Michigan Avenue.

When Conner turned back to face the lake, he watched the sailboats struggle against their ropes and wondered if their moorings would hold. Then the wind stopped suddenly, and the boats sat dead in the water. Their masts like rigid arms pointed up to the sky. When he followed their demand to look up, an azure circle opened in the center of the gray clouds. Mesmerized by the contrast of color and beauty, he stood up and watched a small wispy cloud move into the middle of the opening. It settled directly in the center then stretched like a yawning child, contorting until suddenly it formed the features of a face.

Conner narrowed his eyes and cocked his head. "What the hell?" he asked the sky. While the vivid image looked down at him, every nerve in Conner's body trembled.

"Peter?"

With outstretched arms, Conner stood up and reached to the sky. "Peter!" Conner shouted.

As if hearing his dead brother's name spoken aloud, the clouds rushed to close up the circle. Conner's head began to spin. His vision tunneled, and once again he was being sucked into the black vacuum.

Chapter 4

"Are you okay, Mister? Mister? Hey, Buddy, are you okay?"

The voice jerked Conner from the murky shadows of his mind. When Conner opened his eyes, a weather-etched face was staring down at him. Conner blinked. Concern closed up the fanning lines around the man's faded gray eyes. Conner forced a small nod and shifted his weight onto his elbows.

"Yeah," he answered while trying to shake off what he'd seen.

"You sure you're okay?" the man asked once more.

Pulling himself to his feet, Conner answered, "Yes, thanks. I'm okay."

When their eyes were level, Conner took in the whole picture of this Good Samaritan. Atop a head of greasy, long, salt and pepper hair sat a dilapidated felt hat. Encased in a matching beard, the man's pinched-face was scored with sun-bleached lines. The ensemble was complete, right down to the man's tattered overcoat. Nothing was amiss. Then, unexpectedly, something glinted off the man's lapel. Nestled in the threadbare strip of material was a replica of Ireland's flag, sparking in the sunshine. Conner was about to laugh at how out of place it looked, but then something screamed inside his skull. The pin wasn't out of place. It was exactly where it should be. The laughter he choked back closed up his throat. At that instant, Conner realized that the pin was a confirmation; he had to go back to Ireland, where he'd find the answers he so desperately needed. He had to return to Ireland where it all began.

"But Dad, you don't understand." Conner looked up from his

folded hands at the exact moment Jack stomped by. "I've gotta go back."

Jack pulled up short and snapped his whole body around. "The hell you're going back there! Don't you know what could be waiting for you?"

His father's voice boomed through the Victorian style house and rattled against the floor-to-ceiling bay windows in the living room. It was a beautiful old house, a perfect Norman Rockwell picture when decorated at Christmastime. Conner loved this place. Although he'd always known that someday he'd have to leave, Conner never thought it would be to go back to Ireland.

Conner again dropped his gaze to his hands as he threaded and unthreaded his fingers. "That was a long time ago. I'm sure they've forgotten all about it by now."

"Yeah, right!" Jack snorted while hitching his chin at his son. "And you're willing to spend the rest of your life in prison just to find out."

Standing up, Conner kept the edge of his shoulders lowered and walked toward his father. "Dad, listen, the authorities won't know it's me. I was a kid of ten when you took me out of there." Stopping at the edge of Jack's space, Conner added, "Anyway, they're not looking for Conner Wolfe, American."

Jack's nostrils flared and the veins in his neck pulsated. "Dammit, you get anywhere near Belfast, and someone is going to recognize you."

A single step brought Conner completely into Jack's space. Even though his father angled his dark eyes into his son's blue eyes, Conner didn't back down under Jack's hard glare. Conner knew with all his heart this was something he had to do.

"That's the reason I'm going back. I have to have someone recognize me so I can find out why my father abandoned us and tore my world apart." Conner looked straight into the apprehension in Jack's eyes. "Also, I need answers as to what happened that caused Peter and I to end up in that cave where you found us."

The look on Jack's face made Conner feel as if he was turning inside out. He loved both Cala and Jack with all his heart, and he hated the being the cause of the pain he saw in their eyes. But there were far too many unanswered questions, and Conner knew Ireland was the only place that had the answers.

Jack paused while his fuse burned. "You're still a snot-nosed kid that doesn't know his ass from a hole in the ground, and this proves it!" Jack snapped out.

Cala stepped to her husband's side. She gently placed her hand on his arm and looked up into his eyes. "'Tis a man our boy was that mornin' you came upon him hidin' in the cave with his dyin' brother." The conviction in her voice was wrapped in a rawhide of strength. "Didn't he show, though only a lad, he was man enough to do all he could to save his brother?" Cala gently stroked the coiled muscles of Jack's arm. "And didn't he show you the man he was when, after only a few days, he left his homeland and came with you to the States?" Cala lined a delicate smile at Conner that warmed him. "Now, our son's tellin' us he must be goin' back to Ireland to find the answers he needs."

When she returned her gaze to Jack's face, the softness in Cala's eyes didn't match the determination in her voice. "We're not the ones who make his path for him. We've only two things to do. We accept his decision and love him unconditionally."

The hard line of Jack's jaw sharpened, and he ground his teeth while he glared down into Cala's eyes. "But, I gave him my dead son's name and risked my life to get the boy out of that country." Jack puffed out a long exhale while a pleading look crept into his eyes. "But you were there, you saw what they would've done to him for the part he played in that bombing. If you didn't use your influence with that attorney to help us get the boy a fake passport, God knows what would have happened to him."

There was tenderness in Cala's eyes when she gently cradled her husband's clenched jaw in the palm of her hand. "Yes, I was there when you fulfilled your destiny. You were brought to Ireland to save the boy's life, and you did that. Then together we were to make a happy home for the lad, and we did that. Now our son must find his answers to set himself on his life's path," she said in a velvet voice.

Jack released a hard sigh and lifted a pleading gaze to the priest sitting on the couch. "Tim, please talk some sense into the boy. Tell him."

The priest remained seated, but looked directly at Jack. In the space of Tim's hesitation, shadows of fear and worry shifted through his eyes. Conner knew that Father Tim's love for this family gave him the right to those concerns, but what confused Conner was the pain that laced those shadows. "Cala's right," Tim answered. "You already know my philosophy. God has a purpose for all of us." Tim slid forward in the seat and straightened his spine. "Your son's death led you to Ireland to find God's purpose for you. Now it's the boy's turn. The only way he can do that is to find the answers he needs to help him find his way."

Looking from Tim to Jack, Conner knew his decision was shredding his father's heart, but he had to find the answers. He had to go back. Conner drew in a slow breath. He only hoped those answers hadn't been buried with his brother.

Still looking into her husband's eyes, Cala said, "We don't own our children. They're only rented to us. We're their guides to help them find their paths. We must trust, if not in the Almighty, then in the love we have for our children."

Jack's chin dropped, and his arm encircled his wife's shoulder. A minute stretched out before he turned to Conner and said, "I can't lose you, Niall."

He stepped to his parents. That was the first time in twenty years anyone had called him by his real name. Niall Malone, the orphaned street urchin from Belfast, Ireland. He enveloped his parents in an embrace. "You'll never lose me, Dad."

"You never lose when love's involved," Cala added as soft tears overflowed the rims of her eyelids.

Tightening his arms around his family, Jack asked, "Will you at least wait until after the Fourth of July before you leave?"

Chapter 5

"And ya said he was last here, when?" Daligherat O'Dea asked as she stood on the stone steps and looked over the empty playground. For a moment Di watched the large Irish flag waved from a flagpole at the far end of the chain link fence enclosure. She noticed how the rhythm of her question matched the flapping of the flag nearly perfectly. Di then turned to the man standing by her side

The center's director, Paul O'Sullivan, scratched his short-cropped blonde hair and narrowed his eyes as he thought for a moment. "I'm not sure. I think it was two weeks ago."

Di turned to the playyard and shook her head, not to negate Paul's answer, but to clear her mind. As she searched through her conversation with her brother, the wind gently rocked the swings.

"I was sure his classes ended last week. I don't think he's enrolled in any summer sessions. So I can't understand why he hasn't been here."

Steadying her head, Di turned and looked down into Paul's eyes. "With all the extra shifts at the hospital I've put in this week, I haven't had much time to get here or speak to him. I'm sure 'twas three days ago that I spoke to him. He mentioned that he was busy workin'. I just assumed he meant he was workin' here, at the center."

"Maybe he's acquired a summer job?"

Di rolled her eyes and slapped a sarcastic smile on her face. "Yes, and we both know that's a real possibility."

As she made her way down the steps, Paul's words stopped her at the bottom step. "If ya talk to Marcus, please tell him that the children miss his stories."

Giving the director a short smile, Di answered, "I'll pass that information on, when I speak to him."

Di tossed her sweater over the back of her couch while slipping out of her shoes. As she walked the length of her apartment, she unbuttoned the front of her uniform. She looked forward to getting off her feet after all the double shifts she'd worked. It seemed as if everyone was on summer holiday this past week, and she had run herself ragged trying to keep up with all the extra work.

Slipping out of her clothes and into her bathrobe, she clipped her long hair up off her neck. From her dresser, Di pulled out a pair of soft jeans and her favorite oversized tee shirt and tossed them onto her bed. After a shower, she'd phone her mother and check on the whereabouts of that illusive brother of hers.

As the warm water splashed against her face, Di closed her eyes and let the water work its magic. Her mind drifted to that special place. Suddenly, the fragrance of turf fire and flowers swirled in her head.

She pressed her back to the shower wall and took in a slow deep breath. The water channeled down her body and caressed her skin. His face slowly came into focus and she felt her heart quicken. When his smile widened, she smiled back. The look in his blue eyes warmed her body from deep inside, and Di's lungs shortened. Her fingers thread through her wet hair. She loved him more with each passing day. She sighed.

Then a small flower slowly appeared, and she watched him reach for it. She gave him more than a flower that magical night; she gave him her heart. Every night since, her heart has called out his name. "Please bring him back to me." Di whispered her prayer from behind closed eyes as his face faded into the darkness. She snapped her eyes wide and pushed out a cleansing breath. Her heart knew someday her prayers would be answered. It was her mind that wasn't so sure.

Di finished her shower and dressed for dinner. With bare feet and her hair wrapped in a towel, she moved to the small kitchen. She took out the salad and an opened bottle of wine. Di sat at the kitchen table and poured the wine. She immediately began picking at the salad directly out of the plastic container from the deli. After a sip of wine, she said to her salad, "I'll let me mind go back to him tonight, but for now I'll think about me brother."

After she finished her dinner she'd phoned her mother. During the conversation Ellen O'Dea's voice didn't carry a note of concern. She told Di that Marcus said he'd gotten a job and didn't know when he'd have a chance to get out to see them. However, he did promise that he wouldn't miss Davy's wedding. Di didn't want to ignite any concerns so she gave her mother her love and promised to be at the wedding also.

After Di hung up the receiver, she took another sip of wine. Something about this just didn't add up. Marcus, take a job? She couldn't understand that. He has a real problem with authority, so for him to be working seemed improbable.

Di reached for the phone and punched in Marcus' number. When the machine picked up, she left a message. As she sat sipping her second glass of wine, Di knew her brother well enough to know that the message would probably go unanswered. His dislike for authority extended to an answering machine telling him to do something. Di smiled. She wondered why he even had one.

Finishing the last of her wine, she nodded. Tomorrow evening she'd camp out on his doorstep and get to the bottom of this.

"What are ya doin' here?"

Marcus's voice drew Di's head up from her magazine. She smiled as she lifted herself up to brush a quick kiss onto her brother's cheek. "I'm here because ya don't return phone calls."

"I do too." Marcus's reply was wrapped in his little brother 'don't tell me what to do' tone.

Di stuck out her tongue before correcting her statement. "Okay, so ya don't return *my* phone calls."

Heading up the flight of wooden stairs, Marcus pulled out his key and slid it into the lock. "I returned everyone of yar calls."

She followed him into his apartment and laughed. "Oh, so that little red blinkin' light is yar new disco ball, right?"

Through a scowl, Marcus said, "Shut up."

Making her way around the clutter on the floor and to the couch, Di asked, "So, what have you been up to these days?" Di moved a pile of clothes to one side of the couch and sat down. "Mom said ya've got a job. Does that mean I don't have to send half a year's salary to the university next fall?"

Marcus walked across the one-room flat and opened the refrigerator. He turned to her, holding up two cans of soda. Di nodded and he made his way back through the clutter. Marcus plopped down on the nearest overstuffed chair and picked up his guitar. Marcus strummed the strings, but without the amp, Di couldn't tell if he was hitting the right strings.

He continued plunking as he finally answered her. "That might be the case, since I've no plans to return."

Di felt her anger rushing through her veins. She forced her gaze to move slowly around the room. He'd always been a slob, but living alone seemed to give him permission to let that go to the extreme. She forced a controlled tone in her voice and asked, "Oh, so ya're makin' a large chunk of change, are ya?"

Marcus's fingers stopped for an instant and his eyes shot her with his own brand of anger. "What do ya want from me? Ya want me to pay dues from eight to five as a bean counter? Ya know that's not who I am."

Di pulled herself up in the seat then said, "What I want is for ya to see yar potential and live up to it. Ya've got gifts, gifts that are beyond just intelligence. Ya need to stop throwin' rocks at the windows of yar future and start fulfillin' yar destiny. So stop makin' alibis and get back on track to be workin' on the important stuff of yar life."

Marcus continued to pick the silent guitar strings. "I am workin' on important things."

"So ya're goin' to be a rock star, then?"

Without lifting his head to Di, Marcus answered, "I'm goin' to help people."

"How, by pluckin' yar guitar while those around ya are so drugged up they don't even hear a note of yar music?"

"I'm goin' to work for Ireland."

Di felt her stomach tie in knots. She knew what he was talking about, but she prayed that she wasn't right. "Just how, may I ask, are ya doin' that?"

"I'm goin' to make sure this country is united," he said almost nonchalantly.

Before Di could reply, he looked up at her with eyes that concentrated with desperate intensity and said, "Don't ya see that there's more to life than just the walkin' through it? If we don't grasp the significance of this life, we're lost."

Di wasn't about to let those eyes of his squelch her anger. She flew off the couch and quickly stepped across the room. When she stood with her toes nearly touching his, she said, "What ya don't see is that if ya continue to do what ya're talkin' about, ya're the one that'll be lost."

Marcus stood up and brushed her aside. He tossed the guitar into the cushion of the chair and walked away. "Ya don't understand and ya never will. Ya don't have a clue as to who, or what, I am."

She followed close on his heels. "I know exactly who ya are and what ya're capable of, so stop makin' excuses and grow up." She grabbed his shirt and jerked him around to look up into his face. Di felt anger's lightening exploding in her veins. She shot him with the point of her finger. "Yar logic has run out of reasons, so I'll expect ya to take responsibility and get back to school."

"Ya've no right to be tellin' me what to do," Marcus said, resurrecting his little brother attitude again.

Di didn't take the anger from her eyes. "I love ya and that gives me the right."

"Then love me less and accept me decision as me own," Marcus said as he stormed out, leaving Di standing alone in his apartment.

After a heaving breath, Di walked out the door, slamming it behind her. She stomped down the stairs and mumbled under her breath, "I will always love ya, but I will never accept this decision."

Chapter 6

"Michael Nuggent, ya're makin' me blood boil. I only wanted a few moments of the man's time. I already know it's an impossibility to change the course he's set for himself. What I wanted to do is to stop me brother from doin' somethin' stupid."

Di released the blood pressure cuff and then marked down a few numbers in a chart. She wasn't here officially, but she'd promised Mickey's wife to stop by periodically to keep a close eye on Mick's lungs. When she put her stethoscope into her ears, she motioned to Mickey to turn around. She tugged his shirt out of his pants and listened to his lungs. Mickey's emphysema was getting worse, there was no doubt about that. After making a note in the small chart, Di returned to her tirade. "I want ya to ask the man again, but this time make sure he knows what I want."

"Yar brother is of age. He's the right to make his own decisions. So I'm not askin' anyone a thing on yar behalf, or anyone else for that matter," Mickey said, tucking his shirt back into his pants. "If yar bother wants to stay, then I'll not stop him."

Di stuffed the chart and her equipment into her black bag. "Ya're just as much an idiot as Marcus is."

She made her way to the door and then stopped. "Oh and by the way, stop drinkin' and smokin' or I'll be meetin' the man at yar funeral."

He walked her to the door and smiled. "Maybe then ya'll quit askin' for favors from me."

Mickey stopped inside the entrance of the old warehouse and drew in a hard breath. Lately, the air didn't seem to fill his lungs as it should. What his breath did do was bring in the aroma of stale grease and damp concrete that carried with it memories of the nights in the "clubhouse." That place had been his home from the age of nine to sixteen. Before that, he'd been moved from one relative to another almost every year. When Mickey was born, his mother died. A year later, his father followed her. Most of Mickey's relatives were on his father's side, and none were all too eager to take on another mouth at the table. Mick learned early on that he had to make his own way, so he did. That's how his path directed him to a small band of "lost boys" and how it brought him to this renegade group of Irish freedom fighters.

Walking deeper into the room, Mickey felt sweat trickle down his spine as he forced air into his lungs. Their leader was a heartless man, so Mick just about knew what the answer would be before he even asked the question. Nevertheless, he'd have a clear conscious when he told Di that the man wouldn't release her brother.

When the leader's lifeless eyes lifted to Mickey's face, Mickey immediately posed his question.

"Me friend has asked that her brother be released from the group."

Suddenly, there was life in the man's eyes, but not an ounce of compassion. They spewed out anger that was thick enough to choke on.

Mickey coughed then quickly added, "I'm only askin' because she's a friend."

The man's thin lips curled while he looked long and hard into Mickey's eyes. "I don't care if she's yar whore. Those that join are bound by life."

Mickey dropped the edges of his shoulders and said, "Yes, I know that, but he's just a kid."

The gaunt-faced man threw his head back and laughed. When he brought his gaze back to Mickey's face, the man said, "And ya were how old when ya joined?"

"But I didn't have any family. This kid does."

The man turned his gaze down to the papers on the table. "I'm not concerned with those that might weep at his grave. I have only one loyalty, that's to Ireland."

Mickey turned away and said, loudly enough for the man to hear, "No, it's to yar own murderin' heart."

Marcus was shocked when he went to open the door of the warehouse and the handle turned on its own. Unsmiling, Mickey nodded to Marcus, and Marcus replied his greeting in kind. Marcus immediately stepped aside to give one of the senior members of the group the right of way.

Once inside the warehouse, Marcus quickly stepped up to the table. He coughed. It was done to clear the anxiety from his throat and to get their leader's attention. "I was wonderin' if this time I'll be allowed to come along?"

The man's gaze lifted to Marcus, but without the usual look of irritation lining the man's face. Maybe this time Marcus could be more than just an errand boy.

A small slicing smile slipped over the man's thin lips. "I want ya to divert the one officer that's on duty that day so the package can be left in its proper place. Then ya'll be the lookout and give me a firsthand report of what happens."

"But ya promised the last time," Marcus whined.

Fury shot from the man's eyes. "What ya need to learn is to take orders before ya can give them. When ya learn that, then maybe I'll trust ya to do more."

With a hitch of his chin to the door, the man commanded, "Now get out of here and stop yar bawlin'. I'm not about to have to wipe yar nose or yar ass until ya grow up."

Marcus turned and headed for the door. Anger was quickly replacing his disappointment. Marcus muttered while making his way through the doorway, "When I'm leader, I'll give everyone their chance."

Chapter 7

Conner stood at the window of the hotel room, staring down at the night shadows that danced over the faces of the unfamiliar buildings. Not one sparked a memory to welcome him back, yet Conner's heart knew it was home.

The taxi ride from the airport to the city's center was only a few miles, but it had taken Niall Malone a lifetime to make the journey. Memories pushed his shoulders down. He wondered what waited for him out there. Conner raked his fingers through his hair and settled them at the back of his neck. He massaged the knotted muscles. The city's skyline had changed. Conner nodded in answer to his own thoughts. Both men and cities change, but he knew one thing that hadn't. He released a long slow breath. Twenty years ago he ran from Belfast a scared kid. After all this time, he was still scared.

As the midnight sky melted to a slate gray, the blue lights on Crown Bridge that had kept him company throughout the night were now deserting him. In the street below, the city was waking. Was this city still the same beast that drove his father away and sent his mother to an early grave? Would the monster devour Conner as it had his brother, or would it release the answers to show Conner the path to his destiny?

He stepped away from the window and pulled the dark wool sweater over his head. Conner sneered at the skyline and pushed the sleeves up with a rush of determination. "It's time I face the monster and learn the past of Niall Malone, so I can find the future of Conner Wolfe."

For most of the morning, Conner walked through the gray rain, testing his memory against the street names he'd passed on his way to the East Bridge. There were so many new buildings. If it weren't for the tattered Irish flags on the lampposts, he'd never believe he was in Ireland.

He reached inside his pocket and squeezed the folded paper tightly in his fist. Would the address he'd found in the phone book be the right one, or turn out to be nothing at all? Would he find any of the "boys" or the place they'd called the "clubhouse?"

The moment Conner reached the apex of the bridge, lightening cracked open the sky. A bitter wind kicked up and tugged at his clothes. He buried his head between his shoulders and took off running. A driving rain pelted his face, and the wet strands of his hair channeled small rivulets into his eyes.

A sudden gust of wind shook him like two enormous hands, and he grabbed hold of the bridge's rail. With his fingers embedded in the metal, the tempest sucked the air from his lungs. He choked on the rain that splashed into his mouth. While he was coughing it up, the torrential rain and the squally wind suddenly stopped. Conner slashed his gaze up to the sky. Soft tawny fingers of sunlight scratched a wide blue swatch across the dark clouds. He wiped the rain from his face while he snapped his head in all directions.

"What the...? Where in hell did all the traffic go? And the people?" Conner did a three-sixty turn. The only sound he heard was his heart hammering in his ears. He searched the empty street. Then something moved. He blinked and blinked again. At the base of the bridge stood what looked to be a lean teenage boy with long blonde hair that curled over the collar of his white shirt. Something in Conner's mind screamed for him to run to the boy. Conner raced down the bridge, each step matching the thundering beats of his heart. Then something pulled Conner to a screeching stop. While he forced air into his lungs, he narrowed his eyes and watched as the young man slowly turned around.

Just as their eyes met, Conner heard, "Don't be a cryin', Niall."

Conner gasped and held his breath until it burned. His mind splintered, and he stumbled back a step.

"Peter!" Conner screamed as he raced down the bridge to his brother, his dead brother. As he closed the distance between them, the apparition vaporized.

"NO, Peter! NO!" Conner shouted.

By the time Conner reached the base of the bridge, the vision was gone. An agonizing loneliness drove Conner to his knees. He buried his face in his hands and whimpered out Peter's name.

Conner didn't know how long he'd knelt there or when the rain started again, but when he lifted his head from his hands, the street was once more filled with people and cars. What was happening to his mind? Peter was dead. He died twenty years ago with a bullet in his stomach. The pain-filled memory clutched at Conner's chest. He turned his face up to the sunless sky and allowed the soft rain to wash his tears away.

The door of the building jerked wide. "Pog mo thoin," a slender blonde woman yelled over the ridge of her shoulder seconds before she plowed into the flat of Conner's chest. When her face came up to his, fire raged in her eyes.

Stepping back and cocking his head, Conner said, "Excuse me."

With narrowed eyes, she hitched up her chin and huffed out, "'Tis no use in askin' me that. For I've not the inclination to excuse ya or anyone at this moment. I'm bloody well pissed at the lack of intelligence in this country, and I don't give a fiddler's fart if we're the up and comin' Silicon Valley. We're still a country of people that haven't a lick of sense." Her tirade was said with squared shoulders and nearly all in one breath.

Conner understood most of what she'd said, but maybe not every one of the few Gaelic curses she tacked on at the end. Yet, he couldn't help but smile at how the red stain of anger put a glow in her cheeks.

Still looking over the ridge of her shoulder, she angled her gaze straight into his eyes. "Do ya think us Irish are a funny lot, then? Well, if truth be known, 'tis you Americans that's the real joke of the world."

A swell of patriotism pulled Conner's spine straight. "Now how do ya know I'm not the Irish, like yarself?" he questioned, forcing a heavy brogue into his words.

She snorted out, "Do ya think I'm fat in the forehead? Ya're American 'tis true enough, so ya've no need to be makin' the fun of us with that phony Irish accent." In one swift movement she stuck her nose up into the air as far as it would go and pushed past him.

Holding the door wide, Conner began stepping through the opening, then stopped and called out over his shoulder, "So I guess I should keep the offer to kiss your ass for another time then?"

The woman stopped. He watched as her back stiffened. When her shoulders were squared, he hoped she'd turn and he'd again see that magnificent blue fire in her eyes. Instead, she tossed her head, fanning out the ends of her long hair. With a loud cluck of her tongue, she stomped off. Though a pang of disappointment washed through him, Conner couldn't hold back a laugh.

Chapter 8

Stepping into the narrow, dark hallway, Conner quickly sucked back his laughter. He stood at the base of a flight of old wooden stairs. His nerves quivered. A pain pinched the scar on his cheek, and he ran a grazing finger over it to calm it down. His hands were clammy. He inhaled deeply for strength, then took on the steps two at a time. In seconds Conner stood in front of the door marked with a faded yellow "C." He knocked before he could chicken out.

"Hold yar horses, I'm comin'," the female voice answered seconds before Conner heard the latch release.

A woman with pale eyes set in hollowed sockets and brown hair veined with gray opened the door. Clearly, she was struggling with life from the harder side.

"Aye?" she asked with a curt nod.

Conner pushed a polite smile onto his face before he spoke. "Hi, I'm looking for Michael Nuggent."

The woman curled her lip with her answer, "'Tis me husband ya're wantin'. Hold a mo." She turned her head away and shouted back into the apartment, "Mick, there's an American here to see ya."

A loud hacking cough came through the apartment before the man took her place at the door. His dark hair, trimmed tightly against his scalp, coated his head with a dusting of brown. When the man took a drag on his cigarette, the lines around his dark eyes closed up. The curl of smoke from the man's cigarette drifted out to greet Conner.

"Do I know ya?"

"I'm not sure," Conner answered. "Let me first ask, do you know anyone by the name of Malone?"

After another long drag on the cigarette, the man pressed his hip against the door's edge. Angling his head, he said around a mouthful of smoke, "There's so many of them buggers in Belfast near everyone is knowin' one or two."

"Did you, by chance, know a Niall or Peter Malone?"

There was no mistaking a change in the man's posture and the tightness in his jaw. Yet, there wasn't a flinch in his eyes to prove this was the Michael Nuggent Conner was looking for. "I don't think I've the pleasure of knowin' either man."

"They weren't men back twenty years ago," Conner corrected.

Through narrowed eyes, the man hitched his chin and asked, "Out of curiosity, what might ya be wantin' them for, now?"

"I don't want them. I'm Niall Malone." Conner shot the name out quickly so it didn't have time to riddle him with guilt for deserting him all those years.

While looking Conner up and down, Mickey's eyes widened. There was an unmistakable glint of fear in his brown eyes that Conner caught before it disappeared. Yet, a lining smile moved across Mickey's flat, ruddy face. He quickly stepped aside and swung the door wide. He offered his hand to Conner as he said, "Saints preserve us." Mickey pumped Conner's hand while his eyes flickered down Conner's full length.

"Niall, Niall Malone! How the hell are ya, lad?" The instant the handshake ended, Mickey hitched his head to invite Conner inside. Once he closed the door, Mickey continued to size up Conner.

"How's Peter?' Mickey asked, almost as an afterthought.

"Peter died two days after we left here," Conner answered around the pain-filled memory.

Mickey sighed hard before his gaze dropped to the floor. "'Tis sorry to hear that I am, very sorry. Though I'm not the least bit surprised. There was death's look about him when I put the two of ya on the train that night."

Quickly, Mickey changed the subject and put a smile on his face. "Christ, what happened to ya? How did ya get that mark on yar face? And how, in Sweet Jesus, did ya get to be an American?"

Conner chuckled. "You're the third one to make that observation in the last fifteen minutes."

When Mickey lowered his dark brow and filled his wide face

with a question, Conner nodded with his explanation. "Just as I was coming into the building, a very attractive blonde plowed into me. She ripped me up one side and down the other, then proceeded to make sure I knew just how well-respected Americans are in the world."

Mickey burst out with a robust laugh that he quickly rolled up in a cough. While still struggling to get control of his lungs, he turned away and motioned for Conner to follow him through the apartment.

Conner walked in Mick's wake through the apartment. Narrow windows pinned tightly to the ceiling lit the way into the narrow kitchen. Stepping to the sink, Mickey tossed in his nearly burnt down cigarette, then pulled out a chair. He hitched his thumb for Conner to have a seat at the table. While standing at the sink, Mickey reached up to the overhead cabinet and took out a half-empty bottle of whiskey and two glasses. Without asking, he filled each glass equally and brought them to the table. He placed one in front of Conner. While holding the other glass, Mickey slid into a chair and lit another cigarette.

After a few coughs, Mick said, "Don't be worried about that girl ya met on me doorstep, 'tis only me wife's friend, Di. There's not a thin' that one ain't pissed at these days. So consider yarself in the company of many."

When Mickey raised his glass, Conner wrapped his fingers around the glass in front of him.

"Slainte." Mickey offered the salute, and then drained his glass.

Conner repeated the one-word toast and tossed the liquor down his opened throat. The burn made his eyes water and nearly took all the air from his lungs. Conner gave a small cough while he waited for the alcohol to find its way into his stomach. Once he caught his breath, Conner said, "I'm glad to hear that she wasn't directing that only at Americans."

The conversation carried on into two hours of reminiscing over names and events that were scratchy, to say the least, in Conner's memory. When the stretches of silence lengthened, Mickey lifted from the chair and took a worn brown leather jacket from the pegs on the wall. He punched his hands into the sleeves and said, "Come, let's go to the pub for a pint."

While holding the door open for Conner, Mickey shouted back into the apartment, "'Tis to the pub we're goin,' woman." He closed the door before there was a reply.

As the two men walked up the street, something clutched at Conner's heart. He stopped and lifted his gaze to a large yellow brick building. The setting sun cast an orange glow over the wall of windows. When he read the school's name on the side of the structure, children's screams echoed in his mind. Panic twisted his gut, and fear gripped his heart.

Hatred.

Unadulterated hatred sucked the air from his lungs. How could there be so much hatred in one spot? Conner sucked in the night air to cleanse himself from the toxin that pulsed through his blood.

"Come lad," Mickey called out. "There's a few pints with our names on 'em."

Conner turned and quick-stepped to catch up, but he couldn't stop craning over his shoulder to look at the building. No child should ever have to endure such pain.

Inside the smoked-layered pub, Conner and Mick maneuvered around the clusters of people outlining the length of the long bar. Glasses and bottles littered the glazed surface, marring the reflections of faces that shimmered in the dark wood. The jukebox pumped out country music that filtered over the crowd, yet no one danced. The place could easily be mistaken for one in Chicago. Once again, Ireland tried to confuse Conner. The world was definitely getting smaller. The division between countries was quickly becoming nothing more than political lines.

Just as they walked up to the bar, two stools became vacant. Mick moved into one and gave the universal signal to the bartender for two beers. The moment their two tall glasses of black beer were placed in front of them, a shout came out from the back of the room.

"Hey Mick, who's that with ya?" The thunderous voice easily broke over the noisy crowd. Yet, for a split second Conner wasn't sure whether the pub's conversations stopped to give the question a clear path, or the booming voice made its own way. When Conner turned to the sound, he saw that not only had the voice cut its way through the crowd, but so had the massive man attached to it.

Mickey used the pint in his hand to conduct the introductions. "Francis Boyle, `tis..."

Conner shot out his hand to the bull of a man before Mickey could finish the introduction. "Hi, I'm Conner Wolfe. A friend of

Mick's in the states asked me to look him up, and he was kind enough to invite me out for a pint."

The big man accepted Conner's hand, but kept his eyes on Mickey. "Right, 'tis a mouthful of bull crap if I've ever heard one," Francis said with a smile. "For 'tis well known that Mick doesn't have a single friend in Ireland, nor the States."

Mickey took a sip of his beer before answering, "Well, if that be the case, Francis, me boy, why are ya suckin' up to me then?"

Francis turned to Conner and gave him a quick wink. "I'm a generous man. I feel sorry for yar pitiful soul, Mick."

"No need for ya to be worryin' about me soul. Father Kieran guarantees I've me a place in heaven." Mickey took a hefty swallow of beer, and then licked the foam off his upper lip. "So after I'm a dyin' ya better always be walkin' with an umbrella. For I'll be pissin' down on yar head every chance I get."

A smile cracked Francis's enormous face wide open. "Unless ya piss upwards, I'm a thinkin' I've not a thin' to be concerned with. For 'tis sure I am that ya'll be in hell dancin' to the devil's tune, Mick."

Once he drained his beer, Mickey narrowed his eyes and glared into the empty glass. "If that be the case then I'm sure we'll be meetin' up in the fiery pit." Mickey slammed the empty glass down, putting a clear end to the conversation.

Francis gave a quick nod. With his eyes downcast, he turned and cut a wide swatch through the crowd on his way back to his seat. After dropping onto the stool, Francis sat hung over his beer. There was no mistaking he looked defeated.

Mickey lifted one finger, and the bartender instantly slid another full glass down the bar. With his glass lifted to his mouth, Mickey turned to Conner. "Lad, ya didn't have to be a lyin' to Francis there. True, he's a little *agee*, but though his mind be a might unbalanced, his heart's as big as that head of his."

Conner shook his head. "I didn't lie to your friend. See, I am Conner Wolfe. Niall Malone had to die the night I threw that rock into the pub's window."

Then, as if he needed to tell the whole story, Conner said, "Peter and I rode the train you put us on until he couldn't stand the pain anymore. We jumped off at a small village near the coast, where we found a cave to hide out in. Since Peter had lost so much blood from the gunshot, he was too weak to do much more than lay in his own blood. I tried to find us food. I even stole some right out of the fields, but nothing I did helped Peter. He just grew worse. One morning, I was out searchin' up more things to add to the boil, when an American, Jack Wolfe, followed me back to the cave."

The images in the mirrors behind the bar weren't the haunting ones that reflected back at Conner. What he saw was the face of his brother, cradled in Jack's arms. The gaunt lines of Peter's face were deep and his cavernous eyes even now sent a shiver up Conner's spine.

"Peter made Jack promise to take care of me, and he did. Jack got me out of Ireland and gave me his dead infant son's name. Since that day, I've been Conner Wolfe."

Though Mickey's hand strangled the glass he held, his eyes shifted inside their sockets. Conner couldn't get a handle on it, but something was wrong. His gut was clearly telling him that.

"Ya know, that night, you and the younger lads were nothin' but lapwings to divert the Brits' attention," Mickey said. "Angus and meself had taken that into consideration. We knew yar age would be workin' in yar favor when we planned the bombin'." Mick's gaze dropped, and he stared into his glass. He seemed to be searching for hidden memories. "Those there agreed 'twas a night not forgettin' nor none ever wantin' to acknowledge the rememberin' of it. Maybe 'tis better to leave the past lie."

For a long moment, both men held their silence while the memory of that night congealed in their minds. Conner eased a breath through his lined lips. The weight in his heart lingered, making it feel like he'd just made his first confession. While he took a long slow drag on his beer, Conner watched Mickey's knuckles turn white from the grip he held on his glass. It was clear the memory affected Mickey, but it was more than sadness Conner saw in Mick's eyes. Animals can smell fear; so can a cop.

Mick turned and looked straight at the scar on Conner's face. "Ya never did answer me question about that mark ya're totin'."

Conner raised his finger and followed the line down his cheek. "I was a cop on the Chicago police force. A bust went bad. I got it in the face and my partner and two others got killed. My vision was cut in half by a bullet. So they retired me from the force. That's when I decided to take this trip."

41

Chapter 9

"I thought I warned ya about yar drinkin' and smokin', Michael Finbar Nuggent."

Both men's gazes snapped up from their glasses to the sound of Di's voice.

"Well, now," Mickey answered, "ya did, and that 'tis the truth of it, and I'm followin' yar advice. For I'm not smokin' nor am I drinkin' anymore." Mickey paused for emphasis then continued, "Nor any the less, either." He broke into a laugh so hearty that Conner felt the rumble in his own chest.

Di narrowed her eyes to slits. She gave out with a loud cluck of her tongue. The pinpointed flames in her eyes were like the blue fire of a torch. When she shifted her gaze to Conner's face, he felt the heat.

"And as for you, Mister American, ya needn't be concernin' yarself with the fulfillment of me earlier request."

The laugh that twisted in Conner's throat exploded. He became so wrapped up in it that he'd forgotten his manners and stayed locked to his seat. Mick was on his feet, offering Di, his chair.

"Oh 'tis right, it is," Mickey said with a quick nod. "The two of ya have already met."

Finally finding his manners, Conner jumped to his feet and said, "We hadn't been formally introduced, but that didn't stop her from warmly welcoming an American to Ireland."

"Daligherat O'Dea, Conner Wolfe." Mickey added a wink to the introduction.

When her eyes narrowed, the line of Di's brow furrowed. Then in a blink her eyes opened wide and a smile stretched across her full lips. "Di is easier on the tongue," she said, sliding into the chair Conner had just vacated. With her smile still strongly in place, she gave him a small nod. "Conner Wolfe, 'tis it? So, my guess as to yar nationality was wrong. Ya're the Irish, that's true enough, but ya're more American than the Irish, I'm guessin'."

Conner had just taken a rather swig of his beer and had a hard time swallowing past the chuckle that bubbled up. He extended his hand and said, "It's a pleasure to meet you, Daligherat."

Di cringed at the way he pronounced her name. "I'd prefer that ya'd call me Di. Yar American accent is killin' me name," she said laughing.

Conner smiled with his short answer, "Sure." He released her hand and rephrased his previous sentence. "It's nice to meet you, Di."

Their conversations came in short spurts that they had to squeeze between the waves of cheers and loud music. She spoke with a smile both in her voice and on her face. It seemed to come easily for her. Conner caught her smiling at him even when they weren't having a conversation. For the first time since he arrived in Ireland, Conner felt welcomed back. He was sure it was all because of Di.

During the hour that followed, Conner learned she was a pediatric nurse at Ulster Hospital. She'd also told him that she volunteered her weekends to work at a center for exceptional children. Conner could easily see her with children. There was no doubt that smile of hers would be infectious enough to get many of the little ones smiling back.

When Di glanced at her wristwatch, Conner realized that it was probably late for a work night. Not that it seemed to matter to Mickey.

Conner lifted from the stool and downed the last swallow of his beer. He tossed a few bills on the bar then extended his hand to Mickey. "I should be heading back to my hotel. Maybe we could do this again?"

Mickey hesitated for a second then took the offered hand. "Sure, I'm here most every night."

Conner offered his hand to Di. "It truly was a pleasure meeting you, Di." He winked and added, "Oh, and if you don't mind I'd like to keep that offer you made earlier. It might come in handy sometime."

Di exploded with laughter, and the sound was like music to Conner's heart as he left the pub.

Holding the hand Conner had touched, Di slowly circled her thumb around the center of her palm while she stared at the door. The voices and music in the pub buzzed in her head. It gave her enough background noise so she could separate her thoughts.

He was here. Her heart hadn't stopped tripping from the moment she'd heard his name. After all the years and all those prayers she'd whispered into the night, he's finally here, back, when she needed him most. Her gaze drifted to her hands and she sighed with her smile. Soon it would all be over.

"What's trippin' through yar mind to be puttin' a smile on that face of yars, Ms. O'Dea?" Mick asked over the ridge of his shoulder.

"I'm thinkin' about prayers bein' answered."

"Are ya sayin' prayers in a pub, now?"

"Prayers can be answered anywhere," Di sighed and added, "by anyone."

The lines on Mickey's brow deepened. "Ya're not goin' down that path again tonight, are ya?"

"There's no need to be concernin' yarself with me askin' for a favor again. I'll nay be needin' yar help from now on. Now that himself is back."

Mick nudged his chin at the door. "Then maybe I should be a warnin' the lad that he's the answer to yar prayers."

With the glass just inches away from her lips, Di said over the rim, "There's no need to be worryin' about tellin' the lad. I'll be makin' sure he knows, but it will be doin' him no good a`tall with the knowin' of it." Di turned and smiled at Mickey. "His path has already been set and he'll be seein' 'tis the one that leads to his destiny."

The confused look on Mickey's face told Di he only half understood what she was saying, but it didn't bother her in the least. Niall Malone *was* the answer to her prayers.

Chapter 10

Once outside, Conner looked up at the sky. The moon's full face shined down and added silver to the puddles that dotted the street. A fragrance in the air made Conner's heart ache. The pungent smell of cooked cabbage and boiled bacon layered the streets and brought images of his mother to his mind's eye.

He could see her standing at the stove smiling down at him as he played on the kitchen floor. Her long, curly brown hair and sea blue eyes were still vivid in his memory. Conner sighed. Fiona Malone was a striking woman. As Conner thought of her, he could see that at one time she was probably very attractive. Life wears us all out, and by the time his mother had been taken into the hospital, she had completely worn out. The doctors said it was infection of the heart that weakened her, but Conner knew her heart was broken when his father had walked out. Barra Malone killed his wife the same as if he took a knife to her throat. Conner shook his head to clear these thoughts of his father. As Conner continued to walk through the rain-washed streets back to his hotel room, his mind tinkered with thoughts of both Di and Mickey.

Conner smiled as he thought of the sound of Di's laughter and how it filled him with a comfortable peace. She was easy to talk to. Even in the gaps in their conversation, Conner didn't feel any of the uncomfortable strains you often experience with strangers.

Yet, when his thoughts drifted to Mickey, Conner's smile slid. His life had to have been hard. Though Mickey had no scars that showed, that didn't mean there weren't any. Yet, something in the look Mickey gave Conner was more than the surprise of seeing a ghost from the past. For a moment, fear had cast a shadow in Mickey's eyes. Conner wondered; if he were to scratch at Mickey's guise of friendship, would he find some of the answers he was looking for?

With the damp night air came a flood of memories, memories of the many nights like this that he and Peter spent huddled together in alleyways, their stomachs growling from hunger. As if on cue, Conner's stomach coiled with the memory. He pressed the flat of his hand to his stomach, but it refused his cajoling.

After a few minutes of walking the narrow sidewalks, Conner lifted his gaze to a vacant building directly across the street. Graffiti marred the lower half of the narrow building. The few windows still intact reflected the streetlight like unseeing eyes. Something about the building was familiar.

Conner stared at the dark building for a few ticks of the clock, then suddenly he caught sight of a small silvery shadow playing against the brick wall. It skittered over the surface like a water bug with no pattern or purpose to its movement. At least that's what Conner thought until it stopped at the lintel of the doorway. For a moment, it hung just above the opening. Then, as if it knew it had his attention, it shot up to the top of the building and quickly arced back down in one swift movement. However, this time the silver orb didn't stop at the top of the door. Instead, it disappeared into the concaved entrance.

After racing across the street, Conner pushed his shoulder against the wooden door. It creaked and moaned, echoing into the night. Once inside, he carefully stepped down into the shell of the building.

Panels of blue-gray moonlight cut wide swatches into the dark space, leaving the ebony corners untouched. The impregnated stench of sadness and fear reached out to him. As he sliced his gaze from moonlight to darkness and back again, pictures flashed in his mind's eye. Slowly, Conner turned in place while the phantoms slithered out of the darkness of his mind. Then a sudden realization struck him right between the eyes. This was it, the "clubhouse." The place he and the other eleven boys had called home. His stomach clenched with the onslaught of memories.

"Home." Conner sneered the word into the darkness.

While he continued to turn in place, he couldn't help but wonder what his life would have been like if the events of that night hadn't unfolded. Would he be like Mick, spending his nights with a drink in his hand? Would he be living off the dole? Would he be involved with one of the underground factions, fighting for

Ireland? Maybe he'd be serving up time in Brixton prison, or, worse, he might be in the grave next to his brother.

The wind whistled through the hollowed-out building. The sound reminded him of the many nights muted sobs layered this place. Some of the boys cried because of their empty stomachs, some from fear of being caught and sent to an "Industrial House." Conner slowly shook his head from side to side. That was Ireland's fancy name for orphanages, but everyone, even the boys, knew that's all it was. Their fear of the name wasn't nearly as horrible as the horror stories that came out of those places. Conner shivered. Even today they were still too horrendous to think about.

He turned and walked back out the door. Picking at the scabbed memories wasn't as easy as he'd thought it would be. Yet, he knew he had to clean out the festering wound of his past before it could heal.

The morning sun cut through the window of the restaurant where Conner was finishing up his meal. He sat at the smallest table near the window to have his breakfast. While scanning the Irish Times, Conner wanted to do nothing more than fill in the hours until he could meet Mickey at the pub.

Conner smiled as he looked down at his empty plate. The one thing he really liked about Ireland was breakfast. Back home he'd settle for a quick cup of coffee on the run, but here it seemed to be a sin not to have a plate of bangers and mash.

As he lifted his cup of tea to his mouth, someone tapped on the window. Surprised by the noise, Conner snapped his head up and squinted against the sun. When the dark figure shifted and blocked the sun, Di's face appeared. Conner gave a small wave and a quick smile. She waved back but then was gone.

Before Conner could swallow his mouthful of tea, Di was sliding into the chair across from him. "So, ya're catchin' up on the news, are ya?" she asked with a wide smile.

Conner glanced down at the paper and gave a shrug. "The world doesn't stop when we go on a holiday."

"No, I guess there's no mistakin' that's true," she answered, picking up his knife. Without asking, she took a slice of his toast and slathered butter on it. Conner wrestled with a bubbling laugh and was nearly winning, until she took the second piece. It was then he lost the battle. His laughter bellowed out and Di's head snapped up from her task. She blinked.

Instantly, her cheeks turned to pink and with it came a huge smile. "Oh Lord, I'm so sorry," she said, placing the toast back on the plate. "I'm so used to havin' meals with children that I forget how to act when in the company of adults."

Conner's laugh settled down, but not his smile. "I don't mind. I hadn't intended to eat it anyway."

Di broke a piece in half and took a bite. The way the butter coated her lips with a soft sheen had him thinking how much he wanted to slowly lick it off her mouth and savor the sweet salty flavor of her kiss. He struggled to keep his mind on the conversation, but when the tip of her tongue moved across her lips, he couldn't tell you one word of what she'd said. It wasn't until the waitress came to the table that Conner was able to come out of his trance.

"So what sightseein' attractions have ya been to so far?"

He picked up his check and reached for his wallet. After dropping a few bills on the table, he drank up the last of his tea. Once the mouthful moved down his throat, he answered, "I haven't seen much, got any suggestions?"

Di lifted from the chair and smiled down at Conner. "Well, there's a few spots I find interestin', but I prefer to do sightseein' between the shoppin'."

"Is that where you're off to," Conner asked as he stood up, "to bend some plastic?"

"I thought I might put a slight crimp in it." Di slipped the strap of her handbag over her shoulder and lifted her eyes to his. The blue fire he'd seen in them the first time they'd met wasn't there. Instead, he saw tiny flecks of gold that shimmered in the sunshine. Suddenly, he thought those specks could be even more dangerous than the fire.

"Though I'm knowin' that men aren't fond of such, but if ya're the adventurous type you're welcome to tag along."

Conner chuckled. "Will I have to wear a pith helmet and carry an elephant gun?"

Di smiled with her quick retort. "Not unless there's a sale at Debenhams."

"Are ya sure you can handle them now?" Di questioned as she slipped her key into the lock of her apartment.

Conner looked down at the mound of packages he held and nodded. "Yeah, but what do you need with a gross of charcoal pencils or forty-eight bottles of temper paint?"

Pushing the door wide, Di stepped inside and held it open for Conner. "They're for the kids at the center. School will be startin' soon and they use them up so quickly."

Once he was inside, she turned and closed the door. "I've a few things to purchase here in Belfast. Though the majority of it I'll be gettin' in Omagh, when the store has their before school sale."

The moment she turned back to Conner, she struggled with a giggle as one small bundle slipped from his grasp. While he was retrieving it, two more slipped out of his arms. The sound of her laugher brought his head up and he shrugged and gave her a little boy smile. She fell back against the door with laughter.

"Hey, why are you laughing? Don't you know you're not supposed to look a gift horse in the mouth?"

Between breaths Di answered, "I think horse is a generous term. I believe pack mule is a more true term."

"Pack mule? Damn, woman, them's fightin' words," Conner said as he lifted up from his haunches.

As her laughter continued to ring in the air, Di stepped away from the door just as another parcel slipped out of Conner's grasp. She burst into another round of laughter. "I hope ya're a better fighter than ya are a pack mule."

When at last he had all the packages within the circle of his arms, Conner made a beeline for the couch. He collapsed onto the thick cushions with an exaggerated sigh of relief.

Di walked to Conner and knelt down in front of him. While staring onto his eyes, she slowly began to remove each package and toss them onto the empty space on the couch next to him. With each parcel she took, the pupils in his eyes widened. As she locked her eyes with his, a coiling heat moved through her body. She drew in a slow breath, but nothing cooled the fever spreading out from her core. When she relieved him of the last item, a half smile tilted Conner's mouth. For the longest moment, she remained still, staring into the depths of his eyes.

"There's nothing left for you to take off me," he said, shifting his gaze over her face.

Di widened her smile and answered, "Then me work here is done."

She used his thighs to brace herself, but before she lifted from the floor, he captured her hands. He pulled his rolled back away from the couch and whispered, "I could put them back again."

Giving a quick chuckle, Di slid her hands out from under his and answered, "If ya do, I'll not be rescuin' ya."

Defeat put creases in Conner's forehead and he rolled back into the couch with his reply. "Rescuing wasn't exactly what I was hoping you'd do."

Chapter 11

For the better part of the evening, they chatted over a few beers. The hours flew by, but Conner would have sworn it was only a few minutes. They'd shared their stories. He'd told her parts of his story, the ones about being orphaned and how an American took him to the States, but Conner was careful to dissect the rest.

Di's reaction was more matter-of-fact than surprise. Maybe Mickey told her more of Conner's story last night after he left. He wasn't sure where the line of trust stood between Mickey and himself. Then again, maybe her reaction was nothing more than being polite by not questioning him further.

He'd learned she had a younger brother who was going to Queen's College for his medical degree but decided to drop out for a while. Conner attributed the sadness in Di's eyes to her brother having left school.

"What's true in the heart of one man isn't in the world of others," Conner said. "Maybe he has to find his own path, that's all."

Di nodded, but Conner was sure she didn't agree with what he'd said.

When the conversation slowed, Conner glanced at his watch. "Damn, the time went by quickly." He lifted from the couch and announced, "I should be going."

Quickly, Di unfurled her legs and followed him to the door. Before she opened it, she turned and nodded to him with a question. "If ya've nothin' doin' tomorrow, would ya be likin' a tour of the city?"

Conner veed his brow. "You mean sightseeing?"

Her shoulders came up in a small shrug. "I thought maybe I'd repay ya for bein' me pack mule by bein' yar tour guide."

Conner laughed. "Why don't I think that's going to be sufficient compensation?"

"I'm sure after the trek I'll be takin' ya on, ya'll be seein' that I've more than repaid me debt. Much of the city has changed since ya were last here."

A distant look crept into his blue eyes. Though he wasn't a man who was easily read, for a split second, his guard was down. Inside the wide dark centers of his eyes, she caught a fleeting glimpse of the terrified young boy being dragged away by the *garda*. Her heart ached to erase that memory, but before she could say something, he blinked, and it was gone.

"Yeah, sure," he answered with a small slice of a smile. "What time does the tour bus leave?"

She widened her smile. "How's about I'll be at yar hotel at eleven and we'll make an afternoon of it?"

"Great. I'm staying at the Ten Square."

The day started out wrapped in sunshine, which lightened Conner's spirits considerably. Today, he'd be Conner Wolfe, an American tourist. Tomorrow, he'd go back to being Niall Malone, an Irish fugitive.

Outside his hotel, Conner smiled as he looked down the street. The memory of that fire in her eyes stirred more than a mild curiosity within him. She was an enigma of tenderness and laughter all rolled up in a ball of fire. With the thought of unraveling the mystery of her, he widened his smile.

Sunday traffic was light enough for him to pick out Di's car slowly careening around the few pedestrians jaywalking across the street. When her car stopped at the curb, the muscles in his face felt strained for all the smiling he'd done this evening. Rolling down the window, Di smiled back. With a wink she said, "Top o' the mornin' to ya."

It was the thickest brogue Conner had ever heard in his life. He exploded with laughter and settled into the passenger's side of Di's car.

Once she had the car pulled back into the street, Di said, "There's a few of the regular tourist places we could be seein' today. I thought we'd be startin' at Belfast Castle. Then we can be takin' a jaunt down to the Ulster Museum and enjoy the gorgeous blooms of the Botanical Gardens." She gave him a quick glance and asked, "Would that be to yar likin'?"

Di didn't take her eyes off the road long enough for Conner to get more than a glimpse of the magnificent color in them. A surprising sense of disappointment washed over him.

"Sure, that'd be great. The last time I was in Belfast, I have to admit, I was more concerned with staying out of Tutor House than visiting castles or gardens."

On the tail of a hard sigh, Di replied, "'Tis true enough that I've been known as one that doesn't think kindly about much this country does, but when they closed those orphanages it brought up a rousin' cheer from many, with me included."

He understood where that fire in her eyes came from. It was the zeal of compassion that ignited the flames in her eyes. In Di's case, her eyes were truly the windows to her soul.

Conner's gaze drifted over her. He couldn't help but notice how the softness of her sweater clung to her breasts and the way her golden hair cascaded over her shoulders. He held a smile in check while he thought of how those silken strands would look against a stark white pillowcase. When his gaze lifted to her mouth, he wondered if her lips were soft and tender, or would the raging fire of passion consume the man who kissed them?

"Now, would ya be lookin' at that daft tourist," Di said to the windshield. With a quick honk of the horn, she added, "We be drivin' on the other side of the road in Ireland, ya *eejit.*"

The sharp sound jolted Conner out of his fantasy. He blinked and drew in a breath. Conner hoped his slow exhale would cool the heat rising in him. While he struggled to keep the raging inferno under control, he realized cooling it would take more than a sigh.

When they walked through the doors of Belfast Castle, the contrast between the "haves" and the "have-nots" of the period was evident. There's still a dividing line today between the classes, but it's been dulled by those who managed to make their marks in other parts of the world with little more than the clothes on their backs.

The group of visitors milled around until the short, thin guide coughed. He squared his shoulders and quickly pulled the gold buttons that ran down the front of his blue uniform into a perfectly straight line. Once more, the man cleared his throat, and everyone in the group shifted their attention in his direction.

"Ya're standin' in the third buildin' erected on this spot. The first was built by the Normans in the twelfth century."

Conner bit his lip to keep a chuckle down. The shaggy ends of the guide's gray mustache fluttered with each word. Conner turned to Di, and her eyes danced with laughter. He quickly turned away. Yet, laughter sparking in her eyes was something he knew he wanted to see again.

While the visitors moved about the center hall, the guide continued with his dissertation. "In 1611, the Normans erected a stone and timber castle on this very spot. However, in 1708, while in the ownership of the Chichesters, the buildin' burnt to the ground. We've no record of why the Chichesters changed their names to Donegall near around that same time, but many have their suspicions. In 1870, at a cost in excess of eleven thousand pounds, the third Marquise of Donegall built this present residence."

At the mention of the Donegall name, Conner turned his gaze directly at the guide's face. The man was pointing in an attempt to direct everyone's attention to the coat of arms that hung on the wall. "As ya can see, their crest still hangs in the place of honor on the North wall, and 'tis also the one that hangs over the entrance doors."

Leaning into Di's ear, Conner whispered, "You think he'd trim that mustache, wouldn't you."

Di slammed her hand over her mouth before the laugh could escape. She cut her eyes at Conner and shot him with a warning look that only got her another smile.

When Di returned her attention to the guide, Conner felt pleased with himself for getting that reaction from her. He was about to make another comment, but the group was ushered down the serpentine staircase that connected the main reception rooms to the gardens terrace.

Outside, Conner turned to Di and his breath hitched. With her hair flowing softly over her shoulders, against a backdrop of tiny purple flowers, she looked like a statue of a Greek goddess. The lines of her face were pure perfection, and the fullness of her lips begged to be kissed. She was more than merely beautiful. Helen of Troy had absolutely nothing on Daligherat O'Dea. A lining smile crawled over his lips. Conner easily understood how a man would be willing to sacrifice his life for such beauty. If Di was that beauty, Conner would be the first in line to volunteer his own life.

As if reading his mind, Di turned her gaze up to his face and smiled. Sunlight danced in her eyes, and suddenly Conner was jealous of the sun's fingers that caressed her face.

Di's smile slowly melted as her eyes turned soft. Conner felt he was standing on the edge of a misty blue lake waiting for something to happen, but what? Staring into the crystal pools, he suddenly wanted to spend all his days swimming through the warm currents of her love.

Love?

Where did that word come from? When the word took another turn through his mind, he realized that's what he'd been waiting for, a place where he truly belonged.

"In 1934, the castle was given to the city of Belfast. From 1978 until 1988, the castle went through refurbishment that cost over two million pounds."

Conner blinked at the sound of the guide's voice. He realized his irritation showed on his face when Di gave him a questioning frown. Quickly, he pushed a smile back on his face and stepped to her side. He reached for her hand and casually threaded his fingers through hers. Though he kept his attention directed to the guide, his heart tripped. When she leaned into his side, he released his pent-up breath slowly. Damn, she was beautiful.

Chapter 12

After leaving the castle, Conner and Di hit a few more tourist spots. As they strolled through the displays, they inevitably held hands. The comfortable feel of her hand in his erased the loneliness from Conner's heart. No wonder the word "love" had found its way into his head.

"I'm thinkin' me feet would be likin' a little rest. How's about we head over to the Botanical Gardens where we can stop for a bite?" Di asked, maneuvering the car onto a major artery. "There's many a lovely spot among the flowers that can replenish one's soul and rekindle yar association with Mother Nature, while givin' yar feet a welcomed rest."

The smile she brought up on Conner's face came easy, just as easy as it was being with her. "Sure, sounds nice."

"Both me soul and me feet are thankin' ya kindly," Di tittered.

When she pulled into the parking lot and turned off the engine, Conner turned his face to hers and slid his hand onto her shoulder. She met his gaze with a small surprised look dancing in her eyes. Conner smiled softly while his fingers moved up through the strands of her hair to the nape of her neck. He cupped her head while his gaze moved to her mouth. Her full soft lips drew him closer. Conner knew only a fool danced within the flames, but as he stared into the passion of her eyes, all he wanted was to be baptized within those flames. When the tip of her tongue moved slowly over her lips, a demanding need shot through him.

"I need to kiss you," he whispered through a heavy breath.

She didn't answer, but her breath fanned his face. Conner dipped his head to hers. He had no other intention than to share a tender kiss, but the moment their lips met, that wasn't to be the case. Di's mouth ignited every cell in his body. He wrapped her tightly in his arms, pressing the softness of her to him. Desire raged through him and crashed against his brain. That word was back, but now it vibrated against his skull.

Love. Love.

Conner's tongue slid into her mouth and the womb of the car echoed with his soft moan. When her fingers moved through his hair, he deepened the kiss. Their tongues mated and his body begged for no less. He wanted her with a need that came from his soul. Conner pulled his head back. When the kiss was broken, he forced both his breathing and his body under control. With a deep sigh, he pressed his forehead to hers and whispered through a ragged breath, "Are you for real, Daligherat O'Dea?"

For a moment there was no answer. Then, on the tail of a breath, Di replied, "Aye."

Conner lifted his gaze to her eyes while that single word still peeled in his head.

"Angus, I'm warnin' ya, I'll not be takin' excuses. Ya'll be there tonight or 'tis himself ya'll have to answer to." Mickey seethed into the phone he strangled just seconds before he slammed it back into its cradle. He turned to the window and gazed down to the street below. As he watched a group of boys playing soccer, his mind drifted to the day he'd met the Malone boys.

It was Angus who had brought the pair into the group, and none too soon, from what Mickey remembered. The two looked like they hadn't had a decent meal in weeks. Peter's pale coloring made his blonde hair even more predominant. Though Niall was frail and only nine at the time, there was a look in his eyes of one a helluva lot older.

Peter had explained that they had lived off the streets for about a year after their mam died. When he talked about his father running off, neither Mickey nor Angus was about to share that it was under Barra Malone's direct instructions that his two sons were brought into the group.

Mickey huffed through his nose and curled his lip. The thought of Barra grooming the boys to be the next generation of Irish freedom fighters turned sour in his mouth. Barra hadn't been made the head of the organization because he was stupid, that's for sure. He knew the part the young ones could play, and he didn't care a single bit what happened to any of them. He'd use anyone and everyone he could to get the results he wanted, including his own sons.

Peter and Niall lived within the group for about a year. They all did a little pinching of wallets for cash. Peter was good, but Niall was even better. He had slippery hands and fast feet. Either way, he'd never gotten caught. They were also required to shoplift things they could fence. Conveniently, that fence was Barra himself, but only Angus and Mickey knew that.

The day had come for Barra to start using his little band of bandits for something more than taking a wallet or two. He'd decided to initiate the boys into the world of terrorism with a small bombing on a Brits' boozer. It was a simple plan. The young ones were to ride their bikes and throw rocks through the window of the establishment, paving the way for the older boys to toss "cocktails" inside and take down a few more Brits. That morning, Angus showed Mickey three handguns he'd gotten from Barra.

Mickey shook his head slowly. They were children tossing bombs and carrying guns when they should have been carrying books and kicking footballs. Since no one cared, they followed the one who took the most advantage of them: Barra Malone.

Angus outlined the new plan. Three of the older boys would hide, and, when the soldiers came out of the building choking from the smoke, the boys would pick them off. As Angus told the others, the group's blood boiled with the fever of "patriotism." Mickey saw it in their eyes, each of them believing he was Michael Collins.

It didn't surprise Mick when Angus handed one gun to him, but when Angus handed one to Peter, Mickey was shocked. He knew Angus had gotten his orders directly from Barra, but how could a father do that to his own child? Peter was hesitant to take it, but his loyalty to the group wouldn't allow him to say no.

Around nine-thirty that night, when the pub was packed, the younger lads took off on their bikes with the older boys running after them. The instant the rocks struck the glass, a barrage of gunfire broke out. The Brits were on to them, and in minutes the boys were racing down the street. Guilt filled Mickey's heart and it ached.

Mickey was near when Peter had been shot. Peter didn't scream out. He just folded to the ground with shock riddling his face. The instant Mick realized what had happened, he scooped Peter up and raced back to the clubhouse. Niall was already huddling in the darkness when Mick barged through the door. He screamed for Niall to follow him to the train's switchyard.

Mickey had no doubt that Peter would make it, but Barra had ordered that anyone injured should hop the first train out of the city. Mickey got the two boys on the train and told them to stay on as far as it would take them.

While Mickey stood in the shadows and watched the train pull away, he said two prayers: one for Peter's soul, and the other for his own. Once the train left the yard, Mickey raced back to the clubhouse and waited.

The next morning, he'd learned that some of the boys were already in custody. Even now, Mick felt sick. All he wanted to do was to keep anyone from getting hurt. That's why he'd told the officer the plan.

The Brits promised they'd use only rubber bullets to scare the kids, but that wasn't the case at all. The Brits had decided to make an example of the group, and they didn't care if they were children. Once more, children were used, and again, no one cared.

A few days later, Mickey managed to get to Derry where he settled in and found work on the docks. He stayed for a few years, but he never forgot how he'd been used. As time passed, he came to the conclusion that he couldn't trust either side, but it was better to fight for freedom than to be used by liars.

As a lone man rounded the corner, Mickey took a long drag on his cigarette to draw him back to the present. The family resemblance was uncanny. From the man's sandy colored hair to his long strides, there was no mistaking he was a Malone, all right. Once Niall knew what the name held, would he want it back, or will he keep it buried as he's done all these years?

When Nail knocked, Mickey took another drag on his cigarette and opened the door.

"I see you're ready," Conner said.

"There isn't an Irishman alive that's not always ready for a evenin' of black beer and good conversation," Mickey answered as he slipped on his jacket. While shuffling Conner back out the door, Mickey added, "I spoke to Angus, and he's anxious to see ya again."

Conner cut Mickey a sharp look that struck him dead center. Mick knew where that look came from, so he didn't question it. Angus wasn't one many were fond of being around. Nevertheless, the man had a part to play in this farce, and he'd play it or pay the price.

That night, the pub was near empty. According to Mick, yesterday's crowd was the residue of a local soccer game. Tonight was strictly for the natives.

As they moved into the room, Mick veered to the left, heading to the back of the building. At the end of the bar, Francis Boyle again sat curled over his beer. His only acknowledgment of their presence was a quick slicing glance in Mick's direction.

Mickey tugged on Conner's sleeve and hitched his chin toward a booth, indicating that Conner should follow. Before they were fully settled, a woman with deep lines in her face and near orange hair was taking their order.

"'Tis three pints ya can be bringin' us Annie, me sweet," Mickey said with a wide grin.

"Well, Niall Malone, as I live and breathe."

At the sound of the strange voice, Conner quickly lifted his gaze and found himself staring straight into the eyes of a narrow, chisel-faced man. A thin hand with long fingers shot out to just inches from Conner's face. He took the offered hand but didn't rise from his seat to give the handshake or the man his full respect.

"Angus O'Flynn?" Conner asked, raising one eyebrow.

Angus gave Conner a smile as phony as a three-dollar bill. "That it 'tis, me boy, that it 'tis."

Their handshake ended abruptly. It was clear that Angus had pulled his hand away first. Conner didn't mind. That was the same hand that had given a gun to his brother, so shaking it wasn't high on Conner's list.

"I'm hearin' ya're on holiday of sorts. 'Tis it sightseein' ya're doin', or are ya lookin' up kin?" Angus asked with a quick snapping glance in Mick's direction.

Angus's action didn't concern Conner. What did concern him was the way Mickey tightened his grip on his glass. Conner looked into Angus's brown eyes as he spoke. "Yeah, sorta. Maybe along the way I'll find if Barra Malone is planted in the ground somewhere."

Causally, Mick lifted his beer to his lips while his eyes skittered from his glass to Angus and back again before Mickey asked, "So, 'tis yar da ya're lookin' for then?"

The hairs on the back of Conner's neck prickled. There was definitely something in the look that Mickey and Angus shared. Conner curled his lip and dropped his gaze to his glass. He clenched his jaw as he seethed out his answer, "Barra walked out on us and never looked back. I wouldn't exactly call the man 'Da.'"

While Conner rolled his glass between his hands, he tried to remember when he had begun to think of Barra as being dead. Maybe it started as a wish every time Barra touched Conner with an open hand. One thing's for sure, when Conner heard his mother's cries as Barra coldly walked out the door, Conner had already considered Barra a dead man. The thought of coming face to face with Barra stirred Conner's hatred. His blood ran hot through his veins. Conner realized the years hadn't tempered his hatred for the man. Instead, time had fermented a burn that only revenge could cool. Conner's hands felt sweaty against the cool glass. Revenge? Was that what this trip was all about?

He lifted the glass to his lips and let his gaze skim the rim to settle on Mick and Angus. There was more than normal curiosity in their eyes. Yet, the only question that they asked was if Conner was ready for another round of drinks.

While the cold liquid ran down his throat, Conner nodded. Maybe Barra would be a good place to start the search.

Chapter 13

With the third round finished and a fourth on the way, Mick leaned around Angus and called out, "Boyle, 'tis time, now."

Francis didn't turn to Mick's words. Instead, the bull slowly lifted from the stool and downed the last of his beer. After a small tip of his head to his empty glass, Frances walked out the back door.

"What the hell was that all about?" Conner questioned.

Angus's back stiffened, yet it was Mickey who answered, "There's someone that wants to be a meetin' ya."

"Someone? Like who?" Conner shot out the questions when his cop instincts kicked in. He was sure that "someone" was the Irish *garda*. His heart thundered in his ears as he studied the pair of old friends. There was no doubt Mickey and Angus had been involved in that bombing twenty years ago, but Conner knew all too well the kind of deals cops would make to get "the ones that got away." The fact that the Malone boys had vanished would stick in any cop's craw. Conner knew what he'd do to get a perp, and a softer sentence for information would be the least of it.

Suddenly, the back door opened wide, and the layering blanket of smoke rushed out into the night. The six people sitting at the bar immediately stopped their conversations and turned to the fresh air that swept through the room. After a lengthy second, the clatter of the closing door echoed over the silence. As the sound vibrated through him, Conner prayed that it wasn't the sound of the door closing on his life.

Angus and Mickey scurried out of their seats as four men approached the booth. Only one man slid into the seat across from Conner. The man wasn't dressed in a cop's uniform, but

62

Conner knew that didn't mean he wasn't a cop.

The average built man with thinning sandy colored hair didn't say a word as he stared at Conner. Holding his silence, Conner searched the man's brown eyes. What he saw reflecting in them was empty and hollow, devoid of emotion. Yet, there was something familiar about them.

Conner waited for the chill to finish crawling up his spine then said, "If those two made a deal with you, I hope to hell they got enough for a few pints out of it."

A strange half smile crept across the man's face. "Ya don't recall me then, do ya, Niall, me boy?"

"It's been a while since I've had contact with the Irish police. You'll have to forgive me for not recalling having met you," Conner answered with more his breath than his voice.

"I'll clarify that for ya, then. It was thirty years ago this past April that we met."

Conner snapped his eyes wide while memories ripped through him. "What the hell is goin' on here?" Conner strained his words through tight lips.

"The hell is, I'm yar father, Niall Malone."

Hearing Barra call himself his "father" ignited every cell in Conner's body with scalding fury. He jumped up and drove his arm across the table, slamming his fist into the middle of Barra's smug smile. Before Conner could pull his arm back and do it again, Francis and two of Barra's henchmen wrestled Conner out of the booth and down to the floor. Fists flew, and Conner caught two in the face before he could return a punch.

Barra stood over the pile of men, re-adjusting his jaw. "Let the boy go."

Two men jumped off Conner immediately, but Francis didn't budge. "I said, let the lad up," Barra repeated.

When the bull of a man shifted his weight, Conner pushed the balance of the megalith off him. The second there was space between them, Conner scrambled to his feet. He steeled his gaze at Barra.

"Mick will arrange another meetin'," Barra replied to Conner's silence, then turned and walked out with his entourage in tow.

Conner glared at the closed door through the red hue of anger. Rage twisted his stomach and scaled through his veins.

THE SONOFABITCH WAS ALIVE!

"Ya'll be needin' that bleedin' lip of yars attended to." Di's voice cut through the thunder of adrenaline hammering in Conner's ears. His mind reeled with a mass of questions as he unconsciously walked in her wake out of the building.

Conner mechanically rolled into the passenger seat of Di's car. As his preoccupied mind picked through the few words he'd exchanged with Barra, Conner's ire rose. After several purifying breaths, Conner released a low growl wrapped around a single word. "Father." That bastard had no right to use that word. It was reserved for the man who gave life, not just planted his seed.

Barra's face burned into Conner's mind. He could see the man's sharp nose and his gaunt cheeks, but those cold, lifeless eyes stood out. If the eyes were windows to the soul, then Barra's eyes proved he had no soul. No father could heartlessly walk away from his children like Barra did. No, there was no life in the man to give.

Staring through the windshield, Conner watched the blur of lights and traffic streak by. The multi-colored shards cut through the darkness with no form or definition. Conner closed his eyes and hung his head. When the car pulled to a stop, Conner sat for a long moment staring with chilling clarity into the past.

"Are ya goin' to be sittin' there until the first snow, or are ya goin' to come inside so I can tend to those cuts?"

Without answering, Conner opened the door and followed Di into her apartment. Once inside, she pointed to the couch in a silent command for Conner to sit, then she scurried out of the room.

While reaching into the small black bag that hung on the bathroom door, Di glanced at the mirror. Anticipation had moved up into her eyes. "The wait 'tis finally over," she whispered to her reflection. "Ya've come round full circle, ya have now, Niall Malone. We're together at the apex of it. Soon, all will be as it should be. For none other can do what needs doin' but you, Mr. Malone, and together we'll make sure 'tis done proper like."

Di grabbed some gauze and a small brown bottle and hurried down the narrow hallway. When she reached the archway that led to her parlor, she stopped. Conner sat with his head hung down between his shoulders and his elbows braced on his knees. Her heart sank. There was so much pain behind his eyes, it screamed out to her, and she didn't need to have second sight to know what was going through his mind. She knew if she wasn't careful, all would be lost to her forever.

Straightening her backbone, Di walked into the room. Without hesitation, she knelt in front of Conner, opened the bottle, and poured some liquid onto the cloth. She dabbed it to the cut on his lip. The shock of it got his attention. He sucked air through his teeth and jerked his head back. Tenderly, she took hold of his jaw and drew his head back.

"Oh, stop yar fussin', now." She again touched the small bleeding slice with the moist cloth. "From the looks of it, I think Jimmy O'Donnell was wearin' his face punchin' ring tonight."

When she finished with Conner's lip, she moved to the cut above his eye. After a few passes with the wet cloth, the blood was gone. The scar on his cheek held her attention. She reached up with her finger and delicately traced the jagged red line. "'Tis the mark of a warrior ya're totin'. It will be showin' the devil ya'll not be takin' any of his guff when it comes to those ya're here to protect."

Conner lifted his gaze to hers. "Is that written somewhere, or did you just make that up?"

Di's answer was a smile while she rocked back on her heels. "Now, as part of the treatment, I'd suggest ya stay awhile. Let me switch me hat from nurse to hostess to ask if 'tis a cold beer or a hot tea you'll be wantin'?"

"Thanks, but I think I should leave."

Di knew her face was marked with disappointment, but she gave him a smile anyway. Moving through the door, Conner stopped and turned back to Di. He looked down at her upturned face. "Thanks for the medical attention. I never thought there was any compassion in this city, but you proved me wrong."

On a sigh she replied, "Ya'll find many here that care."

Chapter 14

In bed, with her arms tucked behind her head, Di smiled up at the ceiling. She drew in a deep breath. The lingering spicy scent of his cologne impregnated her mind.

"The waitin' 'tis near comin' to an end. Tomorrow ya'll be learnin' the why of it."

Di bit her lip as she remembered that night twenty years ago. She was five years old and skipping down a torch-lit path. Patches of tiny flowers were scattered along the winding dirt lane. She stopped to pick two small flowers and offered one to a young boy. When he smiled at her, Di felt her heart answer with a silent vow. "I will love you beyond eternity," she whispered to the darkness. They were the same words she'd spoken every night of her life since.

She rolled onto her side and tucked her arm under the pillow. As her eyes slowly drifted closed, she whispered a nursery rhyme to the gray shadows that played on the wall. "One for sorrow, two for joy, three for a girl, four for a boy, five for silver, six for gold." Her voice saturated with sleep, she added, "Seven for a secret yet to be told."

Soft touches of morning sunlight squeezed through the small opening in the drapes as Conner rolled onto his back and pillowed his head in his hands. Staring up at the ceiling, he blinked. His eyes burned from lack of sleep, but his thoughts refused to stop the roller coaster ride they'd taken him on all night.

The thought of Barra being alive twisted in Conner's gut like a red-hot poker. Because of him, both Conner's mother and his brother were dead. Why after all these years would Barra want to meet? Did he expect to be forgiven? As the image of Barra's face burned in Conner's mind, the man's dead eyes sent a chill up Conner's spine. There wasn't a drop of repentance in those eyes. Conner was positive the bastard didn't give a rat's ass if anyone forgave him for anything he did or didn't do. With narrowed eyes, Conner questioned the empty room, "Then why the hell did Barra set up the meeting? Why?" Conner repeated the word. "Why?"

As he continued to glower at Barra's image, it shifted, and suddenly it was Di's face that smiled back at Conner. Damn, she fit perfectly in his arms, and her kiss was intoxicating.

The sudden shrill of the phone jolted Conner around. He grabbed the receiver and lifted it to his ear. On an exhale, he said, "Hello."

"Are you up to the meetin' this mornin'?" Mick asked without a preamble to his question.

Conner tightened his fingers around the receiver. He knew the only way he'd get the answers he was looking for was to meet the sonofabitch. "Where and when?"

"Ten A.M. Two-fifteen West Bank Road."

Without waiting for confirmation from Conner, the line went dead. The room suddenly felt colder. Conner rubbed his bare shoulders and sprang out of bed. After he pulled a sweater over his head, he walked to the window and moved the curtain aside.

Soft white lazy clouds drifted over the blue background. Conner clenched his teeth. Through them he said, "I'll never forgive."

The moment Conner turned the corner, he was flanked by two men in leather jackets. He didn't ask questions, and they didn't volunteer any information. They silently led him directly to an old warehouse. After walking him through a wide door, they moved to the shadowed side of the large space.

The place was essentially empty except for a few crates turned on their sides like seats somewhat lined up a few feet from a long table. The space had the look of a classroom, but Conner was positive the subjects taught here would never be offered in any school.

Barra stood rolled over the table, studying what looked to be architectural plans. He lifted his head as Conner's footsteps echoed in the hollow space.

Shadows etched the deep lines that scored the man's face. "Have a seat," Barra offered, pointing to a crate sitting on its end.

Conner took a hesitant step then sat down. Before he settled in, Barra said, "I'm not goin' to be makin' excuses for me actions. I left because I couldn't be shackled with the likes of a family in me line of work. Now, I'm dyin', and since ya come to our shores I thought to say goodbye before I went."

With his eyes narrowed, Conner slowly lifted from the crate. For a full second he stood glaring hard at Barra's face. Then through sneering lips Conner said, "I hope you rot in Hell."

He turned and pushed past the two henchmen blocking his path. As he reached for the doorknob, a younger redheaded man grabbed Conner's arm. He looked hard into Conner's eyes. "Listen to Barra now, or ya're sure to be sorry."

Conner jerked his arm out of the young man's grasp. Without breaking eye contact, Conner said through his lined lips, "You touch me again you little prick, and you can be sure you'll never use that hand again."

Stepping around the stunned young man, Conner moved to the wide door. Francis Boyle blocked every inch of the opening. Conner turned to Barra and stared in a silent demand. The light that filtered down through the grime-covered skylights marked Barra's face with death's shadows. Yet, Conner wasn't sure if it was Barra's death or the deaths of others that reflected on the man's face.

The redheaded young man walked up behind Conner and shouldered him in the back. "Barra left his family because he didn't want any of ya bein' in harm's way."

Holding his ground against the shove, Conner replied, "That shit don't fly. My mother and brother died because of him. So he can cram that bullshit up his ass, along with you."

The young man quickly stepped into Conner's space. With only a few inches separating their faces, the man smeared on a caustic smile. "Who was it now that put yar mam in that hospital when she was dyin'? And just who was it that sent Angus out to search for ya boys to be a bringin' ya into the safety of the group?"

Conner shifted his weight and leaned forward, shortening the space between their faces even more. Glaring hard into the young man's face, Conner added his own questions. "Who was it that broke me mam's heart so badly that she didn't want to live? If the bastard did bring Peter and myself into the group, who the hell do you think gave that gun to my brother?"

Without waiting for a reaction, Conner stepped around the man and walked up to Barra and spit out, "Do you think I'm one of these brainless underlings of yours? We both know you didn't give a shit if your family lived or died."

Barra's eyes stayed straight; without the slightest hesitation he continued where the young man left off. "Who was it that arranged for that fake passport so ya could get out of Ireland?"

Conner sucked in a quick breath and widened his eyes.

Barra took a step closer. "When Mickey put ya boys on that train, I knew Peter wasn't goin' to be makin' it. I wanted ya both out of the city as fast as possible. I wasn't sure how far ya'd get, but I knew eventually I'd hear somethin'. The first I heard was that a barrister friend of ours was seekin' a fake passport for a ten-year-old boy who was needin' to get out of the country undetected. So I made sure the papers were the best."

Shifting his gaze downward, Barra continued, "That day ya stood in line at the airport, I was not fifty yards away, makin' sure ya got on that plane without any trouble. When ya landed in the States, Father Tim was there so all would go well from that end."

When Barra lifted his gaze, there was a strange calmness in his face that Conner didn't expect to see.

"Every month, I got a letter from the priest with information about ya, with pictures, too." Barra pulled a tattered envelope out of his shirt pocket and shoved it up to Conner's face. When Conner didn't take it, Barra tossed it to the ground.

Conner glanced downward. Nearly a dozen various size photographs laid on the floor at his feet. There he was, looking up at himself from school pictures, birthdays, holidays, his police academy photo, even a newspaper clipping about the drug bust that went sour. Conner stared at the scattered photos. His mind reeled as he tried to make sense of what he was seeing. He lifted his gaze to Barra's face and asked, "Why didn't you say something?"

"What would I have been sayin' back then that ya'd be acceptin'? I'm not seein' a drop of tolerance in yar eyes now, that's for sure. So I'm thinkin', back then, it wouldn't be any different." Barra turned away, and added, "As I said in the beginnin', I'll not be makin' excuses for what I did, and 'tis God, Himself, who will or won't be forgivin' me sins. I'm only wantin' to say good-byes and possibly spend just a little time with ya, nothin' more."

The man's head hung low in a penitent's posture. Slowly, the confusion in Conner's brain cleared. His lungs shortened as his anger rose. "I will never forgive," Conner hissed.

Chapter 15

After leaving a message for Tim to call him, Conner felt claustrophobic and left his hotel. Conner walked the streets for hours, struggling between confusion and ire. The years of respect and trust he'd had for Tim had been erased in a matter of seconds. How could the priest violate the sacred trust and confidence of their friendship? Worse yet, how could the man put a child in such jeopardy? Tim knew that the Irish police could trace those letters back to Chicago. How could he take such a chance not only with Conner's life, but with Jack's also? What could bring a friend to get in league with a devil like Barra Malone?

A cold chill rippled through Conner. Being betrayed by a friend cuts deep into your soul. Barra's words had rocked Conner's world. What Conner wasn't sure of was whether Jack was a part of the conspiracy. If that's the case, then Conner's world wasn't just rocked, it was torn apart. He had to know the truth behind what Barra said. No matter what, Conner was sure Tim would give him that.

Suddenly, Conner found himself standing in front of Di's door.

Barra's hand shook as he swiped away the sweat from his upper lip. His legs trembled, but he willed himself to stay standing.

"You idiot," he shouted out across the hollow warehouse.

His booming voice reflected none of the weakness that racked his body. Every man in the building turned to Barra. Each quickly pulled to attention and stood with wide eyes locked on their leader.

"Ya push me patience," he said as he walked forward. His hand came up and he aimed the point of his finger at the young redheaded minion's face. "Ya're a jackass to think ya could intimidate a Malone," Barra fired out.

With each step Barra took, the younger man's eyes became wider. When their noses were aligned, Barra blasted his words right into the man's freckled face. "The next time ya think before ya put a hand on me son. For it will be more than a hand ya'll be missin'. They'll find ya in the street with a gully stuck in yar ribs and yar blood pourin' into the gutter."

Barra latched onto the younger man's shoulders and gave it a hard shove. "Now get out of me face."

As the young henchman stumbled back a step, Barra lifted his head to the others and said, "All of ya, out."

The group scattered like cockroaches. Once the room was cleared, Barra collapsed onto the nearest upturned crate. He buried his head in his hands and waited as the waves of nausea passed. There wasn't a man among them who could step into his place, but Niall could.

A pain hit hard, and Barra closed his eyes. After gulping a few more swallows of air, the pain began to release its grip. As Barra sat there, Niall's image spread over the back of his eyes. There was still that same defiance in the boy's eyes today as when he was a lad. Barra lifted his head and looked down at his splayed hand. Many a time he used that same hand to keep both boys in line. Though Peter was older, it was Niall who showed the most strength.

Barra gave a caustic smile to the hand he inspected. Today confused the boy, and that would play well into Barra's new plan. His gaze shifted along the bank of grime-covered windows. "I will have ya under me thumb, Niall, me boy," Barra whispered over his curled lips.

"I see the reunion went well."

Barra jerked around to Mickey's statement. Without wiping the sneering smile from his face, Barra said, "Watch yar mouth, Nuggent, or I'll tell me son just who it was that really got his brother killed."

Mickey walked forward without the slightest hesitation in his steps at the threat Barra spit out. "I was thinkin' I'd just tell the whole truth meself and then let him decide who's the one that'll deserve his retribution."

Barra expelled a corrosive laugh while keeping Mickey in his hardened sights. "Retribution, 'tis it? I'm thinkin' the lad will be takin' a gun to yar head once he learns you were the one that told the authorities."

Unflinchingly, Mickey tossed out, "Yar threats mean nothin'.'"

"Aye," Barra said with a shrug, "but what's unimportant to one could be a might important to another." Stepping into Mick's space, Barra curled his arm around the width of Mickey's shoulder and whispered heavily into Mickey's ear, "By the by, how much 'Castle money' did ya get for the tellin' of it?"

Mickey took a step forward and quickly turned to Barra. The look in Mick's eyes told Barra all he needed to know.

"Ya know there was no money given," Mickey said through a clenched jaw.

Barra's smile widened. "Aye, 'tis somethin' I do know, but I'm not sure I could manage to persuade me son of it."

Mickey's eyes rifled fear at Barra, and Barra had all he could do not to laugh in Mick's face.

"Why are ya diggin' all this up now? Ya knew it long ago and still welcomed me back into the fold."

Barra moved to Mickey's side and again curled an arm around Mickey's shoulders. "'Tis true enough, I did know it, but I also knew the knowledge of it would come in handy. I got meself a loyal worker that knows if the information I have is released his life will be worthless. So, I think I'll be usin' this to me advantage." Barra guided Mickey forward as he continued, "Now, as to the callin' cards we need to be leavin' at Omagh."

When Di opened the door, her heart sunk. Conner's face was pale and his eyes were drenched in confusion. "Hi," he squeezed the small word through a sigh.

Di lined Conner a tender smile and replied with her own soft, "Hi." She swung the door wide in a non-verbal invitation for him to come inside. With her back pressed against the open door, she watched him shuffle into her apartment. He carried a heavy weight in his heart.

For a moment, he stood facing the couch as if he was trying to decide if he should sit down or not. After he folded onto the seat, he braced his elbows on his knees and buried his head between his shoulders. As he threaded and unthreaded his long fingers, the rhythm marked the weight of his thoughts. She closed the door and struggled against the need to wrap him in her arms and stroke the lines of his brow smooth.

"I'm sorry, but I a..., I a..., I didn't want to go back to an empty hotel room."

"There's no need apologizin'." She interrupted his stammering explanation. "Ya're always welcomed, no matter the hour." She stepped away from the door as she asked, "Would ya be likin' some coffee, perhaps?"

Conner nodded his answer.

"Black or white?"

"White, two sugars."

In the kitchen, Di mechanically moved through the steps of preparing the coffee while her mind concentrated on Conner. There was chaos behind his blue eyes.

The sound of Di's heavy sigh was lost in the gurgle of the coffee maker. She shook her head slightly from side to side, as she silently cursed Barra Malone. There was no doubt the man was at the center of this, devouring another soul for his own pleasure. Di picked up a spoon and strangled it in her hand. This time there was no way she'd allow Barra to take another man she loved.

Within minutes, Di was back with two steaming cups. She handed one to Conner, then she curled into the empty space on the couch. Di blew the steaming stream away before sipping the hot liquid. She watched how each thought moved through his mind.

Di put a concerned look on her face as she spoke. "I'm knowin' ya'll be sharin' what's on yar mind when ya're ready, but I want ya to be knowin' that I'm here for ya."

She hoped the sincere look on her face would make him see the depths of her compassion. As he gave her a weak smile, he looked into her eyes. She wanted him to see that he could count on her and that he wasn't alone, not this time.

"Thanks, I promise I'll share it all, later," he answered.

They sat in silence as the minutes ticked away. She watched as each thought moved through his mind. When his eyes lifted to hers, he smiled. The guise couldn't hide the pain in his heart.

She returned his smile and then broke the silence. "I've got those supplies to take to the center. Would ya be likin' to tag along and maybe meet the children?"

"Sure," Conner answered with a nod.

Di shifted and unfolded her legs from beneath her. She sat with her back straight and pressed against the couch. "Before we do, I'm needin' to be askin' ya a thin' or two. Are ya knowin' anythin' about Indigo children?"

"Indigo?"

Di pulled herself up as if what she was about to say was important. "Yes, Indigos are special ones that are capable of some achievements. They're so often misunderstood by everyone including the medical community. Then those astonishin' children are misdiagnosed and quickly labeled with the catch-all, A.D.D."

Conner sipped his coffee before asking, "A.D.D.?"

She turned and placed her cup on the table. "'Tis sorry I am to be throwin' medical jargon out like that without an explanation. A.D.D., Attention Deficit Disorder."

"Oh," Conner nodded his understanding.

"But 'tis not the case a`tall. These remarkable children are," Di took a small breath, "are simply more sensitive to the vibrations of the world."

"Whoa, you've lost me again."

"Let me try to explain. Have ya heard how science has proven each of us has an aura around us?"

"I've heard something about it," Conner answered with narrowed eyes. She could see he was clicking back through his mind to remember.

"Well, there are certain people who are born with an indigo color in their aura. They're bright and artistic. However, they're extremely affected by the vibrations all around them. For them, life is like livin' with the speaker of a rock band a pulsatin' through their body. Yet, if these children are nurtured and set on the right path, they can accomplish amazin' feats."

Angling his head, Conner asked, "How do you know so much about these kinda kids?"

"The institute I'm takin' ya to today is for these phenomenal children."

After cocking his head, Conner tucked in his chin and looked down the ridge of his nose into Di's eyes. She slowly shook her head from side to side as she answered his unasked question. "The institute shows them how they're not the minority but are rapidly becomin' the majority. It also shows their parents how to help these children find fulfillment in their lives."

Conner pulled his brow down. "How did you get involved with this?"

"Me brother, Marcus, is an Indigo." Di gave a hard sigh.

"Ok, so what you're saying is that Indigos can get lost in the system?"

"Not only lost, but have permanent damage done to them.

They're drugged, or repeatedly told how bad they are, just so they can be manipulated to fit into a mold of society's makin'." Di set her cup down as she added, "If we don't protect the Indigos, can you imagine what a waste of those gifts they're bringin' us would be?"

"Whoa," Conner shook his head and blinked his eyes. "Wait, backtrack a little okay? I'm still confused. What makes them so special?"

She shifted in the seat and squared her shoulders. "They're special because they're able to do things, like healin' for one."

Di watched as a smirk worked its way over his mouth.

"'Tis true. For I saw it with me own eyes, I did." She added an exaggerated nod to punctuate her statement.

"Maybe it's the cop in me that needs proof. Can you tell me why you believe that?"

Before she began her defense, Di leaned back in the seat and folded her hand. "A siblin' of one of the children was diagnosed with leukemia. When the children heard this, they formed a large circle. While holding hands, they said nothin', just sat there near motionless, with their eyes closed. When they broke the circle, they explained that the child was better now. Not a week later, we got word that the little boy had miraculously gone into remission."

Conner smirked out a tsk with his rebuttal, "But there's spontaneous remissions all the time. What does that prove?"

"That was only the first time. Since then I've witnessed them healin' hurt animals and even the director's broken leg."

"You're shittin' me," Conner said over his slacked jaw.

"Ya see how important they are." Victory danced in her eyes. "'Tis their destiny they need fulfillin'."

The word "destiny" got Conner's eyes to snap wide, but he asked, "Does Marcus help out at the institute, too?"

"No, these days he's found another interest." Di said as she stood up. "Would ya be likin' to go to the institute now?"

"Sure, I'd like to see those 'miracle kids' of yours."

Di chuckled out, "Just don't be shocked if ya're findin' that description to be true."

Chapter 16

The building was airy with a soft shade of blue painted on the walls. Large windows captured enormous quantities of light that illuminated even the farthest corners. Children, from toddlers to teens, moved from room to room at will. A group of seven or eight-year-old children sat at a bank of computers while others stood at easels creating paintings. Near the window, a small circle of younger children looked to be enjoying the pictures in the books they held nestled in their laps.

Walking deeper into the room, the display of students' artwork that decorated the walls caught Conner's eyes. They ranged from impressionist to landscapes, and from what little he knew of art, the paintings looked to be very good.

A young boy with tawny hair looked up from the book he held. "Hi, Miss Di."

Immediately, Di stepped up to the circle and lowered onto her haunches, leveling her face with his. She greeted the boy with a wide smile. "Hi, Anton. What are ya doin' today?"

"Nuttin' much, just little bit of readin'," the boy answered. He held up a book on the life of Da Vinci.

Di gently closed her fingers over the boy's small shoulder. "Leonardo is a fascinatin' subject."

After she stood back up to Conner's side, he whispered, "That's a big book for a little guy like that. Yet, he seems to be enjoying the pictures."

Di's eyes glinted with amusement. "Anton, this is me friend, Conner Wolfe. Mr.Wolfe is from America, but he's interested in the book ya've got there. Would ya like to share a bit of it with him?"

Anton nodded his small head before lifting the large book into a reader's position. "Leonardo Da Vinci had a keen eye and quick mind that led him to make important scientific discoveries, yet he never published his ideas. He was a gentle vegetarian who loved animals and despised war. As contradiction to that, he worked as a military engineer to invent advanced and deadly weapons. He was one of the greatest painters of the Italian Renaissance, though he left only a handful of them completed."

"Holy shit," Conner whispered under his breath.

"Thank you, Anton. 'Twas kind of ya for sharin' that." Di took a few steps forward but stopped and turned back to the little boy and lined him a fain questioning look. "Oh, by the way Anton, how old are ya now?"

Without lifting his head, Anton answered, "I'm three."

Conner caught Di's reigned smile before she turned to head in her original direction. He felt his jaw slack as he watched her walk away. Conner had heard about kids that bordered on genius but never came face to face with one.

When Conner realized that Di was already a few steps ahead, he raced to catch up with her. Before he could get his steps in cadence with hers, a little girl with big blue eyes rushed up and tugged on the sleeve of Di's jacket.

"Miss Di?"

Di immediately lowered to the little girl's level. "Hello, Elizabeth." Di's voice was the softest Conner had ever heard.

Without saying a word, the auburn-haired child stretched out her small arm and handed Di a flower. Di cradled it in her hands like a tiny bird. "Why, thank you. That's very sweet."

Suddenly, the image of a blonde-headed girl offering him a flower drifted into Conner's mind. Di came up and slowly nodding as a delicate, lining smile touched the corners of her mouth and spread into her eyes. "Yes. I was the one who presented ya the flower that night in Tirnageata."

Conner widened his eyes and sucked in a breath. "Oh my God. You? Why didn't you say something when Mick introduced us?"

"I wasn't sure how ya'd respond to the knowledge."

Conner looked deep into Di's eyes. "You can't imagine how many nights I dreamt of that little girl."

Di released a small breath with a single word, "thanks."

The softness of her smile held his attention longer than he'd planned. The need to hold her overwhelmed him. He turned away to break the draw. As he did, his gaze struck a group of teenagers sitting around a table.

"What the...?" He cut his sentence off to edit his word. "What are those kids doing there?"

"They're doin' a bit of readin'," Di answered in a matter-of-fact tone as she moved in the opposite direction.

The mixed gender group leafed through the pages of their books faster then Conner could blink. "That can't be reading."

"'Tis amazin', isn't it."

In the center of an adjoining room was a table covered with tiny resistors and printed circuit boards. While one boy carefully placed a bead of solder on a circuit board, two other pre-teens huddled over a motherboard as if performing an intricate surgical procedure.

Conner snapped his head around to Di and asked, "They're not taking it apart, are they?"

"Och no, they're building it," Di answered casually as she waved to one of the girls that glanced her way.

After inhaling a long breath, Conner slowly exhaled. "This is just too goddamn unbelievable," he said, without regards to editing.

"Miss Di?" a brown-haired, brown-eyed boy of about eleven shouted out as he raced across the length of the room.

Di immediately stopped. "Yes, Frank?"

"I spoke to me sister last night. She told me Tiger was with her."

"So ya've no need to be worryin' then, now do ya," Di answered as she gently patted the boy's short-cropped hair.

The look on Frank's face showed a hint of relief, but there was still a mark of deep sadness in his eyes. "No, I guess not, but I miss them both."

She wrapped her arm around his shoulder in a tender hug. "I know." When she released him from her embrace, Di said, "But ya can talk to them whenever ya want, so 'tis like havin' them with ya." The boy added a nod to his unsmiling face and raced back to the easel and his painting.

Di restarted her trek through the room. When she and Conner were a few steps away from the nearest group, she whispered, "An Indigo talks to the dead. Five years ago, Frank's sister was one of the victims of the Shankill Road bombing, and now his cat disappeared a few days ago."

Conner snapped his gaze over the line of his shoulder at the boy. "Does he know he's talking to a dead girl?"

"Yes, but he wouldn't tell anyone outside of the institute. Here, he knows he's safe."

When Conner and Di were nearly at the door, he noticed a tall, lanky teen sitting alone. "Why's that kid sitting all by himself?"

Di turned to the boy Conner had referred to. "Each Indigo has different traits, very few have them all. The ones that do, know the level they're at."

"I see, so he's sorta the big shot around here."

"Somethin' like that."

"So, you're saying that they don't all have the same abilities."

"That's right. Most didn't know what they were. Many are still fightin' against low self-esteem. Yet, some, like Robert," Di hitched her chin in the boy's direction, "knew long before anyone else.

"Can ya imagine," Di said on a sigh, "how many more are out in the world tryin' to understand why they're different. Think of the sufferin' they're goin' through."

The instant the teen's chestnut head came up, a strange tingle crawled up Conner's spine.

"Miss Di," Robert called out.

"Yes, Robert?"

"Would ya and the gentleman come here, please?"

Di's eyes asked Conner's permission, and he nodded his reply. "We'd be happy to."

"Hello, I'm Robert Jameson."

The young man stretched out his hand to Conner. Conner stepped forward and shook the teen's hand. "It's a pleasure to meet you. I'm Conner Wolfe."

Conner's palm instantly warmed. As the heat intensified, He struggled not to jerk his hand away, and instead he consciously forced himself to pull his hand away slowly.

"Are ya joinin' our group?" Robert asked.

"No," Conner chuckled out quickly.

"Why not? Ya're one of us."

Conner gasped before he answered, "I don't think so, Robert."

"I'm never wrong," Robert said, putting in a long pause before finishing his response, "Conner."

The hesitation Robert added before saying Conner's name had Conner sucking in a quick breath, while he stared into the boy's mesmerizing brown eyes.

When Di threaded her fingers through Conner's, the spell was broken. He snapped his gaze to her face and slowly released his pent up breath. A delicate smile tipped the corners of her mouth upward and a light moved into her eyes. Conner gently squeezed her hand. Life was always throwing him into darkness, but something in her eyes told him this time he didn't have to go it alone.

"There's a little place around the corner that serves up a great ploughman's lunch. Are ya rememberin' what that is?"

"Irish stew, thick enough to stick to your ribs, or fill a pot hole, right?" Conner chuckled out.

Di joined in with a giggle as she teased, "Or we could go back to my place for a black puddin'."

Wrinkling up his nose, Conner answered, "Let's check out the stew."

While they made their way through lunch, Di could hear how purposefully Conner kept the conversation away from Robert's comment. She followed Conner's lead and didn't push. Yet, she knew how vital it was that Conner didn't lose sight of the whole picture. The kids needed for everyone to know about them, but her brother's life depended on Conner knowing.

Di dabbed at the corners of her mouth to hide the smile that bubbled inside her. "I know what ya saw today could inspire many a question. Yet, ya seem to be satisfied with just what ya've seen. Still, with ya not makin' a single comment about what ya saw, 'tis a question I have for ya."

She paused and watched how the spoonful of stew he lifted stopped just inches from his mouth. Tension ripped in the air, and she forced herself not to smile as she continued, "Was me earlier appraisal of those miracle children accurate?"

Di wasn't positive, but she thought he released a small sigh of relief just a second before he took the spoonful of stew into his mouth. She was sure that his head nodded in silent confirmation.

"'Tis glad I am that ya grew up smart enough to know that a woman's right ninety-nine percent of the time."

Conner's eyes blinked, "Well, what about the other one percent?"

It was a struggle to keep the laughter down until she finished what she had to say. "Och, men are no good a'tall with deflated egos, so we give them that one percent to keep the smiles on their faces."

His laughter erupted full force and rang out around the crowded pub. When the melodious sound faded, Di felt an emptiness wash through her. Laughter feeds the soul, but his was a feast for hers.

After a few spoonfuls, Di said to her bowl, "I've been invited to a weddin' Saturday next. I was wonderin' if ya'd be interested in joinin' me."

"Sure, as long as I don't have to wear a tux," Conner answered without hesitation.

Di lifted her gaze to his face. She needed to gauge the impact her next sentence would have on his decision. "Only a clean jumper is all that's ever required for a weddin' in Tirnageata."

Conner stopped the spoon just inches from his mouth. His eyes opened wide, but when he added nothing more to the conversation, she immediately added, "I wouldn't be invitin' ya back if there was the slightest chance of a problem. We've all known there's secrets that need keepin', so ya needn't be worried if there'll be a problem." Di held her breath in anticipation.

"I think I've got a clean sweater for the occasion," Conner finally said.

Silently, Di released her pent up breath with a soft sigh. He accepted her first request, but would he accept the second?

As the sun washed orange into the sky, Conner finally understood where this comfortable feeling around Di had come from. She was the little girl, the one in his memory whom he had carried with him all his life.

Di smiled as she said, "Would ya be likin' to come back to me apartment for coffee?"

Conner returned her smile and nodded his answer. He threaded his fingers through hers and led her out to the sidewalk. A few feet away from the pub, Conner drew their joined hands up and noticed how perfectly they fit together. He understood his feelings. Being with Di felt like coming home. When his gaze shifted to Di's upturned face, his heart tripped. The way the dying sun shimmered in her eyes took his breath away.

"I'd never seen blue fire until I looked into your eyes." He gently ran the back of his fingers down the line of her jaw then leaned to brush a soft kiss over her mouth. The moment their lips met, he wanted to melt her to him. He wrapped her in his arms and hungrily took possession of her mouth.

The sensation of her soft body pressed against his fed the demand raging through him. Conner's hands moved down her back and over the round of her backside. Gently, his fingers kneaded Di's taut muscles while he imprinted his hardened body to hers.

When her lips parted, a low guttural moan vibrated in his

throat. His mind was drugged by the hot moist cavity of her mouth.

"Whoa, ya two need get yarselves a room before ya're arrested."

Conner ignored the passerby's comment, but when he heard the whistle that followed, he broke the kiss. He pressed his forehead to hers and waited for his breath to level out. "I think it might be better if I caught a cab back to my hotel."

"Maybe 'tis a good idea," Di replied, fighting against her shortened lungs.

He pulled back and smiled as he corrected, "I didn't say it was a good idea, but it's probably a smarter one." He kissed her forehead, then added, "For now, anyway."

After helping her into her car, he watched the two red taillights move through the traffic-lined street. Conner turned. "Tirnageata." He exhaled the word as he wove his way through the crowded sidewalk. His sketchy memories of the town included picturesque whitewashed cottages nestled on a patchwork quilt of various shades of green, a rugged coast outlined with jagged cliffs, and the cave where he and Peter had hidden. These were what Conner remembered of Tirnageata.

When a cutting wind blew through the crowd, Conner drove his hands deeper into his pockets. He was sure there wasn't much about the small hamlet that wasn't beautiful, except one thing. It was the place where the two Malone boys had died.

Chapter 17

A ringing phone greeted Conner as he opened the door to his hotel room. He dove across the bed and quickly lifted the receiver. "Hello."

After shrugging out of his jacket, Conner reached for the lamp next to the bed and turned it on.

"Hi, Father Tim, thanks for returning my call," Conner said then slowly drew in a breath to steady his anxiety. On a slow exhale, Conner said, "Father, I need you to tell me all about your association with Barra Malone."

Silence came through the wire. It held center stage in the long distance conversation for a full minute. Then in a strangled voice Tim said, "I've been waiting for this call since you left for Ireland. I'll tell you anything you want to know, but I'd prefer to do that in person. I'll catch the next flight out."

The strain in the priest's voice was something Conner had never heard before. From the first day they'd met, Tim quickly gained Conner's respect for both the collar and the man behind it. Through the years the priest had been like a second father to Conner. Yet, after what Barra said, and the pictures he produced, all that Conner had believed seemed to have been wrapped up in lies. He knew the priest deserved a chance to explain. Conner also knew it was the respect he had for the man that would give his friend that opportunity. Conner's heart ached.

"Thanks, I'll be waiting" were the only words that found their way out of Conner's tightening throat.

Tim gently replaced the receiver into its cradle. He pressed the flat of his hand against the tightness in his chest. As the hurt in

Conner's voice echoed in Tim's ears, the air in the room became heavy. How could he explain what he'd done so that Conner would understand? He'd always believed what he was doing was on the side of angels, but hearing the pain in his young friend's voice made Tim question his motives. What he'd done could be construed as wrong, but nothing had been done with even an ounce of malice.

The priest lifted his gaze to the window across from his desk. The sky was the most magnificent summer blue he'd seen since he was a child. This is what every child should have, a life of endless summer sunshine in which to play and grow. Those thoughts didn't lighten the weight in his heart. He was positive about one thing: What he'd do again in a New York minute. As he confirmed that in his mind, Jack's face appeared in Tim's mind. The priest knew that whatever he'd say to Conner would have to be done face to face. Tim had too much respect for both Conner and Jack to not explain in person. Tim stared at the cradled phone as he wondered if he should go to Jack and give him the explanation first. "No," Tim said to the phone, "I'll tell Conner first."

Tim pulled out a tablet and started to outline the things he wanted to say. Each time Tim jotted something down, he'd quickly scratch it out. This continued until he had a full sheet of nothing but crossed out lines.

"Father Tim, dinner's on the table," the housekeeper said as she slowly pushed the mahogany door open.

"Thanks, Mrs. Foley. I'll take it a little later," Tim replied.

Truth was, lately his stomach hadn't been too eager to have food in it. After Conner called Tim, what was in there was going to try to get out. Tim put his pen down and rubbed his temples. He had to find the words that would show Conner how important their friendship was.

Conner walked with his shoulders rolled against the damp, chilly night. As he reached the crest of the East Bridge, he stopped to look up at the sky. The sharpened points of the stars glittered against the black velvet.

All that Barra had said was true, at least that was Conner's take on it after the quick phone conversation he'd had with Tim. Even though Barra had saved Conner's life, it still stuck in his craw that Tim had betrayed him.

While Conner stared up at the stars, a vaporous cloud floated across the moon. It twisted and curled then fell from the sky down onto the surface of the water. The cloud then unfolded like a flower opening its petals. Out of the center, a misty shape began to take on a human form. The congealed apparition, held in a gossamer pair of hands, skated over the top of the water then stopped. Conner gripped the rail with both hands, embedding his fingers into the cold metal.

"Peter." Conner whispered the name with a ragged voice.

The vision rose up from the water, leveling itself eye to eye with Conner. Peter smiled, and the tension in Conner's heart eased.

"Ya'll be knowin' the right path, Niall."

The words in Conner's mind were locked behind the lump in his throat.

"Ya'll know the right path," Peter repeated.

Conner's mind spun. "I don't understand what you mean." When the vaporous image dissolved and drifted back over the water's surface, he leaned over the rail and shouted, "Please, Peter! What do ya mean?"

As Conner held tightly to the cold metal railing, tension rippled up his arms and coiled into the muscles of his neck. He trembled as he stared at the glazed surface. "How do I know what's the right path?" Conner questioned the still water. "How do I know?"

Chapter 18

"Are you sure the couple won't mind me crashing their wedding?" Conner asked, lifting the two suitcases from the car's trunk.

"A weddin' in Tirnageata isn't a formal affair. The church might overflow some, but a crowd only makes the occasion more joyous," Di answered as she tried to take her bag from Conner. He was about to add a scowl to his silent refusal, but the smile that lit up Di's face was contagious.

Instead, he returned her smile and slowly shook his head from side to side. Who was this woman and how did she hold such power over him? Was it the promise of a kiss on her lips that shackled his heart, or was it the way she felt in his arms? What he knew was that his body wanted her. He diverted his eyes in hopes of controlling the primitive fire coiling through him. When their eyes met, a spark flinted and he felt his control slipping. Suddenly, Conner hoped to hell she hadn't lied about not being an Indigo. He didn't want his face slapped for the thoughts that were racing through his mind.

Di winked and turned to lead the way to the house. Conner quickly gathered up the bags and followed her down the stone path and up onto the narrow porch. Before Di had a chance to knock on the cottage door, it swung open wide. A slender, angular woman rushed out and warmly greeted Di.

"Oh, darlin'," Ellen O'Dea said as she enveloped Di in a tight hug. Brushing a kiss onto her daughter's cheek, Ellen said, "'Tis so grand to be a seein' ya."

The mother-daughter moment was cut short when Ellen shifted back and smiled at Conner. "Why Niall, ya've grown into such a handsome, strappin' lad, ya have."

Conner wasn't sure how to respond to her greeting or to her calling him Niall. He simply turned the scarred side of his face slightly away and returned her smile. "Hi, Mrs. O'Dea."

"Ya're near family, Boy-o. 'Tis no need to be callin' me anythin' but Ellen." She encircled both his and Di's waists and ushered them into the house. "Now, come, settle in. I've put the tea to boil."

Inside the house, the mouth-watering aroma of sweets baking gave an aromatic welcome that caused Conner's stomach to answer. Yet, it wasn't just the delicious fragrance that greeted him. There was a love in the cottage that reached out its arms to him, and suddenly Conner felt a pang of homesickness.

He looked around at the yellow painted walls. One was near covered with the faces of smiling children at various stages of growing up. He smiled back. Before Conner could examine them more closely, Ellen nudged her chin in the direction of a small stairway tucked in the corner of the kitchen. "Ya'll be bunkin' upstairs with me son, Marcus."

"Is he here yet?" Di asked with a quick glance around the room. When her gaze met Conner's, he caught a hint of urgency sparking in her eyes.

Just then the teapot whistled and Ellen moved to answer it. "Aye, as Davy's best man, 'tis Marcus's duty to be helpin' the boy calm his weddin' jitters down at the pub."

Di chuckled out, "Let's hope they don't become too calm and not be a showin' up for the ceremony."

"No need to worry. Da's there to insure they get to the festivities on time," Ellen answered, spooning loose tealeaves directly into the boiling water.

Di motioned for Conner to follow her up the stairs as she laughingly asked, "And who is it now, that's to be a keepin' an eye on Da?"

Ellen's laughter followed them up the stairs.

After showing Conner where the bathroom was and which room he would be sharing with her brother, Di stepped to the room across the hall. Before she closed the door, she gave him a half smile and a wink. Conner laughed, knowing that it was more of a tease than an invitation.

Shafts of sunlight cascaded through the stained glass window and sent a shower of multi-colored prisms to dance atop the heads of the congregation. The white runner, stretching down the center aisle, was sprinkled with colorful confetti shapes of light that continually shifted like an ever-changing expressionist painting.

Conner and Di sat in the last pew and watched as the old stone building filled with people. When a family of eight filed down the narrow aisle, Di leaned against Conner's shoulder and whispered, "Margaret and Danny McMichaels use the 'awareness' method of birth control."

"Awareness?"

Without turning to him, Di answered, "Yes, they're well aware of birth control, but they're not into practicin' it."

He coughed to cover his laugh as his gaze drifted over the crowded church. It was just as Di predicted. The number of people did overflow the church and quickly spread outside onto the steps. Yet, not a face in the crowd looked agitated to be there. This was a place of peace, and the people of this hamlet clearly knew the value of the gift they possessed.

At the altar, a gray-haired priest stood on the highest step, waiting to begin the ceremony. The cleric's white and gold vestments looked strained against his stocky frame, but his smile was definitely a welcoming one.

Soft murmuring voices stirred through the delicate music of the organ and harp. The subtle melody didn't interfere with the hum of the conversation. It actually accentuated it.

After a few minutes, the melodious tune was replaced by the haunting tones of a single bagpipe. The bold music drew the guests' attention to the groom and the best man who moved to the foot of the altar.

Though the crowd blocked Conner's view of the two men's faces, he saw parts of the pairs' attire. Obviously, their matching black jackets stood out against the white walls of the church. However, their dissimilar kilts caught Conner's eye, as did the best man's flaming red hair. Once the two men were in position, the piper slowed his tune and the organ took over again.

The rich musical tones introduced three small girls dressed in identically matching yellow gowns, each with a colorful plaid that slashed across their small chests. With solemn expressions and total concentration on the flower petals and sprigs of holly they tossed onto the white runner, the girls marched to the altar.

Once the little girls finished their trek, the music again made a change. This time, the sweet refrain of the harp's rolling strings spread through the building like a prayer. Then the doors to the church opened wide and everyone shifted in their seats. All eyes were as wide as their smiles as the soft awes of the congregation's approval matched the notes of the harp. The bride regally stood framed in the wood of the doorway. Two older women made final adjustments to the folds of the bride's pale blue gown and to the ringlet of tiny white flowers atop her long sable hair. After a minor adjustment to her flowing sleeves, all the fussing stopped. The bride pulled her back straight. With her shoulders squared and a ribbon-tied bouquet of twigs and small flowers cradled in her arm, she waited.

For a stretched out moment, the bride looked directly at the altar, then she stepped forward. All inside the church lifted from their seats and watched as she floated down the aisle. When the bride reached the foot of the altar, her groom took her arm and together they knelt before the priest. Conner blinked when he saw she wore no shoes.

With a bible hugged to his chest, the pale-faced priest looked out over the crowded church and announced, "Today, we're here to witness the marriage of Laura and David." He took their hands and helped them rise.

When the bride and groom finished saying their vows, Conner glanced at Di. Glints of sunlight shimmered in her golden hair like captured fireflies. He wanted to rake his finger through the length and release them.

As if she heard his thoughts, Di turned to him. She smiled and threaded her fingers through his. Her mesmerizing smile held him captive while the lure of her eyes drew him deeper into their crystal blue pools. When the music reached a crescendo, Conner's heart swelled with it.

Di's attention moved to the bride and groom as hand in hand they happily hurried back down the aisle. Conner turned to the couple with a smile already stretching the muscles in his face. Yet, as his gaze struck the best man's face, Conner's smile fell sharply.

Barra's redheaded underling!

Conner narrowed his eyes. What the hell was going on? While the question stomped through his mind, Conner held the man's face in his beaded sight. The man's smile brightened as he looked at Di, but instantly changed to a wide-eyed look of shock when his eyes locked with Conner's.

Di leaned into Conner's shoulder and asked, "Doesn't me

brother look handsome in his finery?"

With a quick breath, Conner snapped his head to Di, but her concentration was on the little girls racing out the church.

"Brother?" Conner asked on a heavy exhaled breath.

"Yes," Di beamed. "Though 'tis Davy's day, I believe Marcus truly is the best man."

Di's brother?

The little prick was Di's brother, her Indigo brother.

Conner stared at the top of Di's head. The hairs on the back of his neck lifted. Did she know that Marcus was working for Barra? He did remember her saying something about her brother finding other interests. Was that the "interests" she referred to?

Di smiled up at him and Conner tried desperately to put a smile back on his face, but it wouldn't form. He pushed out a long heaving sigh and turned to watch Marcus melt into the crowd.

Chapter 19

The hurry to follow the bride and groom out the church caused a bottleneck at the door. As Di and Conner stood waiting to step out from the pew, every person who passed Di offered her a smile or a kiss. When there was a break in the exit line, Di moved into the aisle and motioned for Conner to fall in behind her.

Instead of the usual receiving line outside the church, everyone followed the newlyweds to a clearing across the street. While Di led Conner to the group, he visually searched the crowd. There was no sign of Marcus anywhere. Conner had expected Di's brother to find a way to avoid Conner, but he didn't expect the guy to vanish. What concerned Conner even more was whether Di and her family knew about Marcus' association with Barra.

The guests formed a circle around the happy pair. Once everyone was in place, Ellen O'Dea walked into the center. She pulled the hood of her long coat up to cover her head and smiled. A tall, impressive man followed on her heels, also adjusting the hood of his cloak to cover his gray hair. They stood before the new husband and wife and addressed the gathering. "Welcome."

In unison, everyone responded, "Welcome."

With up-lifted arms, Ellen and her companion petitioned to the heavens. "Oh Great Spirit, we ask for your blessin' on this ceremony."

Dipping his head down to Di, Conner asked in a heavy whisper, "What's going on?"

With her eyes locked on the ceremony, Di cupped her hand to the side of her mouth. Directing her whisper to his ear, she answered, "'Tis the way a weddin' was done by our ancestors. Me mother and Henry Byrne are the Druidess and Druid of the village."

Di's gaze lifted to Conner's face. Her eyes danced with laughter as she added, "No need worryin'. Me mam wouldn't be changin' ya into a toad."

A smirk slipped over his mouth as Conner huffed out a breath through his nose as a reply.

When Ellen lowered her arms, Henry kept his outstretched as he said, "Let the power and radiance enter our circle for the good of all beings. May the harmony of our circle be complete."

When Henry lowered his head and his arms, Ellen stepped forward and took hold of the couple's hands. She placed the bride's small one atop the groom's larger one and held their hands captive between her own. After sharing a private smile with the pair, Ellen lifted her head and looked out over the gathering. She announced, "We stand upon this holy earth to witness the sacred rite of marriage between Davy and Laura. As the family and friends of Davy and Laura come, we ask the greater power to be present within our circle."

Henry moved forward and sandwiched their hands in his. He smiled at the couple as he added, "By me power, I invoke the God of love whose name is Aengus Ma Og to be present. In his name is love."

Ellen turned to Henry and replied, "By me power, I invoke the Goddess of the bright flame whose name is Brigid to be present. In her name is peace."

After Henry removed his hands, the others followed. Ellen lifted her arms and eyes to the skies as she petitioned, "We ask the spirits and souls of our ancestors to accept this union of your children."

She paused, taking in a long breath as her gaze moved to Conner's face. Speaking directly to him, she continued, "Help them, guide them, and protect our children. Keep them on the right path."

An electrical surge pulsated through Conner's veins. His lungs shortened and his heart thundered in his ears. He lifted his eyes to the heavens just as a cluster of silvery clouds gathered into a shape of a warrior's shield. Sunlight filtered through the center and cast a circle of light down to the graveyard behind the stone church.

"Are ya feelin' ill?" Di's whispered question caused Conner to blink. When he reopened his eyes, the gossamer image had disappeared. Unable to push his answer out through his tightened throat, Conner silently shook his head from side to side.

Though the ritual continued, Conner's restless mind wasn't following any of it. What just happened? Why did the channel of light beam down to the graveyard, and was Ellen really talking directly to him?

Suddenly Henry's voice cut through Conner's thoughts. "The sacred rite of marriage ends in peace, as in the peace it began. Let us withdraw, holding peace and love in our hearts until we meet again."

A combination of whistles, cheers and applause exploded throughout the clearing as the newlyweds kissed. Di was smiling and clapping along with the others when she glanced at Conner. "'Twas a beautiful ceremony, wasn't it?" she asked with joy-filled eyes.

However, Conner could only work up a small smile and a nod in reply.

The newlyweds rushed off down the street, with the crowd close on their heels. Di started to follow the group, but Conner tugged on her sleeve. "What's happening next?" he asked.

"'Tis time for the celebration at the pub."

Conner looked across the street at the iron gate of the cemetery. He knew he had to search out Peter's grave.

"Can I meet you there in a few minutes? I have a stop I need to make."

Questions raced through Di's eyes, but they were never asked. Instead, she slowly nodded and walked to the tail end of the group. On her way, she passed Ellen and Henry. Di said a few words to both of them, and then shared a hug with Ellen. Ellen turned back to Conner and nodded before she and Henry joined up with Di and the others.

Conner walked across the street and followed the stone path around the back of the church to the graveyard. As he moved from headstone to headstone, he tried to remember which was his brother's grave. Conner's memory was hazy. Hell, he was just a kid when the town secretly buried Peter, so he could understand why he didn't remember. The only time Conner had seen the grave was the morning he and Jack left for the States.

Panic crept in, but Conner reminded himself that he'd find it. Then, as he stepped over a ground level grave marker, a flat headstone with a single angel carved on it caught Conner's eye. There was no name engraved on the gray marble. Conner's heart quickened. That was it. He moved to the graveside and knelt down on the damp grass. A shiver shook his core, but he reached out his hand and slowly grazed his fingers over the embossed angel.

"Oh Peter," Conner sighed aloud.

Unshed tears burned in Conner's eyes as his fingers moved gently back and forth over the cold stone. "I've missed you," he choked out through his tear-clogged throat. "I've missed you so much." Conner curled his fingers and dug his nails into his palms as he fought for control. "Why did you have to be the one to die?" Conner shivered. "And why am I always the one left?"

"The one left behind is always the strongest."

Conner was startled by the soft sound of the voice. He snapped his gaze up from the stone to the woman standing across from him.

The tenderness in Ellen's eyes caressed the grief in Conner's heart. She looked directly at the scar on his face and gave him a small smile. "Ya know our ancestors believed a scar won in battle was a magical thin'. 'Twas said to be a shield from the evils of his enemy."

Conner drew in a long breath and slowly exhaled. "Yeah, but this shield is a dark one. I walked away with a hole in my face when the others never walked away at all."

Ellen stepped around the grave and knelt down at Conner's side. She curled her arm over the width of his shoulder and held him close. "Then 'tis lucky ya are."

He struggled to keep his tears from stealing all his words. "Surviving when others around you die isn't luck."

"Then yar destiny must be an important one." Ellen brushed a kiss on Conner's forehead. "For ya wouldn't have been saved for nothin' that wasn't, now would ya?"

Conner looked into the woman's face. Suddenly, he was ten again, standing at the crossroads of his life. "I'm not sure what my destiny is."

"Och 'tis sure I am, that when it comes, ya'll be a knowin' the right path," Ellen answered with a smile. Conner offered her a smile in return, but he still didn't know the right path.

When she lifted up from her haunches, she guided Conner with her. "We've a weddin' to celebrate. How about dancin' with an old woman?"

After Ellen linked her arm through his, Conner replied, "I have to warn you, I'm not very good."

Ellen patted his arm and chuckled out with a wink, "Doesn't matter, lad. I'm the best dancer in the county, so ya'll not even be noticed out on the dance floor."

When Conner and Ellen walked into O'Brien's pub, they were greeted by a toe-tapping jig. Ellen waved at the orchestra and a tall thin man playing the skin drum blew her a kiss. She quickly pulled Conner onto the dance floor and together they spun the narrow length of the room. When the tune finished, she wrapped her arm around his waist and led him off the dance floor.

At a nearby table, Di sat smiling up at Conner. "I see ya had a whirl on the dance floor with Mam."

Conner shook his head and smiled. "She's more like a whirlwind."

"'Tis no better dancer in the whole county than me Ellen here." Coming up behind Ellen, the drummer wrapped her in a big bear hug that lifted her off her feet. Ellen feigned a struggle, but the giggle in her voice said she wasn't really trying to fight him off.

As Conner turned to Ellen's giggle, he stood nose to nose with Marcus. There was a look of fear sparking in the young man's eyes. It clearly begged Conner not to say what was tramping through his mind.

Standing up with a wide smile that had spread into her voice, Di began the introductions. "Conner Wolfe, the man attackin' me mam is me da, Thomas O'Dea." When Tom winked at his daughter, Di responded in kind.

Quickly, Conner extended his hand to Di's father, who took it. "How do you do, sir."

"The last time we met, ya were a scrawny kid," Tom said with a smile as he pumped Conner's hand. "Looks like America agrees with ya."

Di stepped to Marcus' side and looped her arm through his. She looked up to his face, then said, "And this strappin' lad 'tis me brother, Marcus."

Conner didn't want trouble, not here, not for Ellen, not for Di. Di turned her gaze to Conner. There were glints of sadness and concern mingling in with a sister's affection in her eyes. Conner swallowed back the anger from his voice and extended his hand. "Nice to meet you, Marcus."

A look of relief washed over the young man's face as he took

Conner's hand. "'Tis a pleasure meetin' ya, Conner." The hesitation Marcus put before adding Conner's name was similar to the space Robert used when he greeted Conner at the Center. Conner still wasn't sure why Robert hesitated, but there was no mistaking why Marcus paused.

Tom brushed a kiss to Ellen's neck and took hold of her hand. "Will ya take a spin on the dance floor with me, me love?"

"I'd be honored, husband mine."

As the couple laughed their way onto the dance floor and blended into the crowd, Marcus turned to Conner. "Thanks for not mentionin' we've met previously."

Within a blink, Conner snapped his gaze from Marcus to Di. He tried to read the lines in her face before he asked, "You know what he's involved in?"

When she nodded slowly, Conner felt his heart sink. "Aye," she replied on the tail of a sigh.

The twist in his gut moved up into his stomach, and Conner suddenly felt sick. He searched Di's eyes for any hint of compunction, but there wasn't even a single drop. Conner tried to keep his lip from curling, but it was no use. He nudged his chin at Marcus, while never taking his eyes off Di. "And you condone what he's doing?"

Di pulled in closer to her brother's side. "Marcus knows me feelin's about the situation."

Watching Marcus pat the arm she had resting on his, Conner's anger rose and heated the back of his neck. He pushed out a long puffing breath and hitched his thumb in the direction of the dance floor to help get his question out. "I'm safe to assume your parents don't have a clue what the hell you're up to, right?"

Marcus shifted his weight and unthreaded Di's arm from his. Again, fear sparked in his blue eyes as he answered, "They do not and I'd be greatly appreciative if ya didn't go tellin' them."

Conner watched as Ellen and Tom glided through the crowded dance floor. They didn't deserve that crap in their lives. Then, looking directly into Di's eyes, Conner spit out, "Don't worry. I'll keep your dirty secret, but I'll have to say that you're both pretty goddamn stupid."

Then Conner speared Marcus with his gaze. "You, for the pain you'll bring to your parents." Conner turned his full anger onto Di. He sucked air through his teeth as he glared down into her upturned face. "And you," he pushed his breath back out through his teeth, "for allowing him to get involved in that shit." Conner shook his head and turned to the door. As he walked out of the pub, Di called after him, but there was no reason for him to stop.

Chapter 20

The chill of the night air had no effect on the heat of Conner's anger as he stomped across the field. Pain-filled memories ripped from his heart and brought back the horrific images of his dying brother.

Marcus and Di had to be shown that violence wasn't the cure for this fragmented country. All it did was feed the addiction to death for people like Barra. Just then the man's face flashed in Conner's mind. The lifelessness in Barra's eyes was proof that nothing good ever came from spewing carnage out into the world.

Conner balled his fists inside his jacket pockets and turned his gaze up to the sky. Thousands of tiny stars shimmered in the night sky, and each took a turn winking at him. He couldn't stand their joy-filled rhythm, so he quickly dropped his gaze to the darkened tree line. Silver moonlight caught on a path that cut its way over the field. Conner was sure he knew the way to the O'Dea's house, at least he did in the daylight, but he hadn't remembered seeing that road before. He stopped and turned in place. The lights from the town were over his shoulder, so he knew he was heading in the right direction. When he took a step, the wet cuff of his jeans slapped against his leg. Conner looked down at his feet. "Okay, time to get off the wet grass."

He'd only been walking down the road a few minutes when he realized he'd made the wrong choice. He turned back toward the town but pulled to a quick stop. "What the...?"

The moon's soft gray light washed down on the head of a young girl sitting on a rock wall. "Where did you come from?" he shouted out as he walked toward her.

Each step he took brought more of the teenager out of the darkness. With her face still in shadows, the girl's long, thick, curly hair cascaded past her shoulders. Her crossed legs hung only a few feet down the waist-high stonewall, so Conner knew she couldn't be more than five feet tall. When he took another step, a cat meowed from the darkness of her arms.

"Sssshhhh, Tiger," the girl said as she stroked the cat's head. "'Tis no need to be frettin'."

"I didn't see you sitting there when I walked by before."

"I saw you."

On a slow turn in place, Conner said, "I'm sorta lost. I know the O'Dea's house is down that way." He pointed his finger in the direction he thought the house was as he said, "But I can't seem to find it."

"'Tis just down the path to the left at the first fork."

Squinting his eyes against the night, Conner tried to remember if he'd passed a fork in the road or not. Before he could mentally retrace his steps, the girl climbed down the wall and came over to stand by his side.

"I'm goin' in that direction, so I can keep ya company on yar journey, if ya'd like."

"Sure, that'd be great."

The girl stroked the cat's head and began a barrage of questions as they walked along. "Ya're an American, aren't ya? What's it like to be a livin' in the States?" Conner was about to answer her first two questions when she fired another one at him. "Are ya here for the weddin', now?"

"Yes," he quickly broke in. "I'm here for the wedding and yes, I'm an American. But, I was born in Belfast, and it's great living in the States." Conner added a chuckle as he matched the speed of his answers to her questions.

When she turned her head up to his, moonlight shimmered in her eyes. He noticed that she looked past his shoulder, and suddenly Conner felt as if something was watching him. Quickly, he turned in the direction she looked, but there was nothing there except the black shadows of the rolling hills that melted into the night sky. When Conner turned to the girl, he caught her long curls still bouncing from the quick nod she gave in silent answer to an unheard question.

"Are you okay?"

Her eyes snapped to his. "'Tis nothin' amiss with me, sir."

"What were you looking at?" Conner gave another quick glance over his shoulder and back again.

"The night."

"But you were shaking your head like you were answering someone."

"I'm havin' no other conversation but ours at the moment."

Conner angled his head while he searched her shadowed face. Her lining smile showed just enough teeth to confirm she was smiling. He smiled back, but a jumpy feeling spiked against his nerves. Suddenly, the cat hissed. The animal's eyes reflected sparks of moonlight from the darkness of her arms.

"Your cat doesn't seem to like people much."

"Tiger likes me and me brother, Frankie, well enough, and an occasional stranger."

"I guess I'm not one of those strangers."

"I wouldn't be sayin' such. She hasn't tried to scratch ya yet, so ya're on her short list."

Conner chuckled but didn't dare put the girl's conclusion to a test. Instead, he moved on to another subject. "So what are you doing out here all alone?"

"I was on me way home from the fishmongers on Shankill Road."

"Shankill? That's in Belfast. That's a far way for a kid your age to have gone alone, isn't it?" Conner questioned.

"Here's the fork that'll take ya to the O'Dea's," she said quickly.

Did she ignore his question? Conner wasn't sure, but he didn't push the issue.

"Take care to be stayin' on the road," she added "Bogs are everywhere, so I wouldn't be driftin' off the center, now."

He stopped and looked down at the top of the girl's head. "How about I walk you home? I don't like the idea of you out here at night, all alone."

The girl looked down the divided road as she answered, "'Tis kind of ya to worry, but there's no need. I'm bein' met." She pointed into the darkness and excitely bubbled, "There he comes, now."

Conner searched the black horizon when a tiny light pricked the darkness. Slowly, the eerie light bobbed and swayed as its beam skimmed the surface of the crawling fog. The steady rhythm of the undulating blanket moved as if the earth was talking in slow breaths. As Conner watched the light's movements, once more the edges of his nerves quivered. He pulled his collar up and shifted inside his jacket.

As the girl raced to meet up with her escort, the fog stirred but strangely not from her movement. Instead, it seemed to swell and shroud the pair, leaving only the light to move deeper into the night.

"Thanks again for your help," Conner called to the shrinking yellow spot.

"Ya'll be knowin' the right path now, Niall," the girl's voice echoed out of the darkness.

He turned to the road and took a step, but stopped suddenly as his brain registered what she'd said. When Conner snapped back around, the pair and the light had vanished. Peter's voice reached out from the creases of Conner's memory. "Ya'll be knowin' the right path."

Conner stood at the side of the road straining his eyes against the darkness as thoughts spun in his head until he felt dizzy.

As the headlights of Di's car found Conner standing on the side of the road, she said a quick prayer of thanks. Once she had the vehicle aligned with him, she rolled down the window and said above the motor, "Get in."

Lines of confusion scored his face, but the condemnation that was in his eyes at the pub had disappeared.

When he didn't answer, she added, "There's thin's that need tellin', so please, get in."

Conner opened the door and slid onto the seat. He gave her one quick glance then turned his attention to the rear window as the car took off.

While they moved over the twisting, narrow road, Di struggled to find the right words. She knew the only thing he'd accept right now was the truth. How could she get him to listen to it all before he stormed out again? More so, if he stayed, how would she get him to agree?

Di pressed down on the gas pedal. She had to get into the house where the walls could protect her when she bared her soul with the truth.

The minute the car pulled to a stop, Di was out and walking up the stone steps well ahead of Conner.

Inside the dark house, shadows moved around the room. Di stood in the moonlight, unsure if she should turn on a light. Then she realized that Conner had to see the truth on her face. He deserved that. When she switched on the lamp, she saw him standing at the window staring out at the night.

Di lowered to the couch and pinched the bridge of her nose. "Ya've got it wrong, ya know. I'm not condonin' what Marcus is doin'. I'd begged him not to be a part of that, but nothin' I said could change his mind."

She massaged her temples. Her head ached, but it was her heart she was worried about. Di looked up and stared at the width of Conner's back. His spine was rigid and his head slowly moved along the dark horizon. There was no doubt he was building up a wall. All she could do was pray that he'd stay long enough to hear the whole truth. She drew in a ragged breath for strength then pushed it out.

"After I found out, I was plenty angry. For the longest time, I'd only be talkin' to Marcus when our parents were about. That's when I realized how thin the fabric of time was. I'd no right to be a wastin' even one precious second of it bein' angry. Then I began thinkin' of a way to go around Marcus, so as to accomplish the same end. 'Tis when I devised a plan to be showin' Barra how important ones like Marcus were to the world. I tried to enlist Mick's help but that was a hopeless cause. Not only was Mickey against it, but yar father flatly refused to give me an audience."

Conner jerked around and glared down at Di. She watched him chew his words before she jumped in. "I know ya're not considerin' Barra yar father, but he does."

Di uncoiled from the couch and moved to Conner's side. His eyes flashed in a clear signal to keep out of his space. She obeyed and turned to look out the window. "When all attempts failed, I began prayin' for someone to come and set Barra on the right path.

"Right path?"

The strain in Conner's voice brought her face to his. She searched his eyes, hoping to find something she could hold onto. What she met was confusion mingled with...with what? Shock? Was he shocked by what she'd said? It couldn't have been because the look seemed to come from something deeper than her words.

As if he didn't want her to see, he quickly turned back to the window.

She turned to the darkness, but then closed her eyes. It wasn't the night's vista she sought, but strength to tell him all. "I prayed. Yes, I prayed and it was you that was sent."

With a wrinkled nose and narrowed eyes, Conner gave his rebuttal, "I'm here not because of your prayers."

"Ya're the one that was sent to intercede."

Di felt the heat of her anger rise into her cheeks. Her finger came within an inch of his nose and she seethed, "Who ya are is the one that was sent to help." Di realized she'd said that with more determination than she wanted. She puffed a heaving breath through the line of her lips. Alienating him wouldn't serve her cause, so she pushed her anger aside.

She then placed her hand on his arm. Tension rippled through his muscles and up into her fingers.

"You've got it all wrong. I'm not here to do anything but find out who I am. I wasn't sent to help you or your brother."

"Yes, ya can," she said calmly. "All I'm askin' is that ya explain to Barra what ya saw at the center. Tell him the importance of each one of the Indigos, including Marcus."

"He's not going to believe that stuff happened, let alone care."

"He'll care if *you* explain it."

"You're thinking the man has human feelings. He didn't give a shit about his wife or kids, how in the hell is he going to care about your brother?"

"You can convince him. I know ya can," Di pleaded.

"Even if I do get him to understand, what good would that do? Marcus has his mind set to be a part of the problem."

Di knew she was far from getting Conner on her side, but this was the break she needed. She thought all she had to do was give Conner the pure facts and he'd surely put his weight behind her. "Yes, that's true, but if ya get Barra to agree, then he'll be expellin' Marcus."

Conner jerked his arm from her hand. He stood looking down his nose at her. "What you don't realize is that Marcus will just find another faction to join."

Hearing the hopelessness of her cause spoken out loud ripped open her heart. Di buried her face in her hands. "But ya're the one to help. I know it. Ya were sent in answer to my prayers. Please, please, ya must save his life," she choked out between sobs.

Conner gathered her into his arms and tried to soothe the tears that racked her body. The only word he heard was please. The only answer he gave was yes.

He kissed the top of her head and stroked her back. She looked up at him with eyes soaked in wet. When he brushed a kiss over her lips, the mixture of bittersweet tears and the softness of her mouth clouded every thought but one from his mind. He wrapped her tightly in his arms and deepened the kiss. When their tongues mated in the ancient ritual, every cell in his body screamed with need; the need to touch her, the need to taste her, the need to bury himself deep inside the warmth of her.

Together, they folded to the floor as his hands and mouth took possession of her body. He moved his lips down her neck and dipped his tongue in the hollow spot at the base of her throat. His trembling fingers opened the buttons of her blouse. The feel of her skin against his finger was like warm satin. He splayed his hand over her breast and gently kneaded his fingers into the soft tissue. Her hardened nipple pushed against his palm and he hungered to draw it into his mouth. When she released a sigh into his mouth, he imprinted his body to hers.

"Make love to me. 'Tis our destiny," Di's whispered words were wrapped in a ragged breath, thick with passion. "'Tis always been our destiny."

Before her words were melted in the heat of his passion, they flickered against his brain. Conner pulled back and looked down at her kiss-swollen lips. What was she doing? Worse, what the hell was he doing?

"You better button your blouse," he said as he rolled away. He struggled between the need of his body and his conscience. He wanted her, but not as payment for his promise. "You don't have to prostitute yourself."

Di sat up and held her blouse closed with both hands. Her wide eyes slashed over Conner's face. "But...but."

"Don't worry," Conner spit out as he lifted to his feet. "I'll talk to Barra, but it has nothing to do with destiny. I'll do it because your parents deserve better than you and your brother. But you two are all they have and I couldn't live with myself if I didn't do what I could for them."

"But...but ya're...wrong," Di stuttered.

Conner was upstairs before she could finish her sentence. He couldn't stand to look at her, but worse he couldn't stand how his body still wanted her even after he knew what she'd do for her "cause."

Tim's nerves hadn't stopped quivering since he'd received Conner's phone call. The priest pressed his hand over his heart to slow it down, but nothing helped. He'd said a silent prayer to find the right words and for strength to say them. Whatever was said in the next few hours could destroy a friendship that the priest felt was as close to a son as he'd ever have.

The priest had been a part of Conner's life from the moment

Jack brought the boy to the States. Tim felt that the opportunity to be involved in every facet of Conner's life was a gift. He shared holidays, special occasions, and all the days in between with the Wolfes. When Conner had asked Tim to be his sponsor for Confirmation, Tim was beyond proud.

Tim shifted forward in the overstuffed lobby chair and tried to rotate his left shoulder. Lately, it had been aching. He knew he should have stayed in his room to wait for Conner, but he didn't want to move from this spot. Conner could walk in any minute, and Tim felt he had to be there when Conner did.

Rolling back into the chair, Tim picked up his newspaper. He scanned the stories as his mind stumbled through a clutter of thoughts. The achy joint in his shoulder wouldn't allow him to concentrate. He pulled himself up and shifted again in his seat until he sat rolled shouldered over the newspaper.

Chapter 21

The minute Conner entered the hotel's lobby, he came to a quick stop and stared. Tim sat rolled-shouldered in an overstuffed chair, reading a paper. The man of strength whom Conner had left in Chicago four days ago was not the same man sitting in front of him now. Conner watched as Tim shifted his left shoulder. The priest was carrying a heavy weight, there was no doubt of that.

Conner stepped up to the priest with an outstretched hand. "Hi Father, when did you get in?"

When Tim snapped his head up, his face was scored with deep lines and his blue eyes swam in a sea of red.

"I caught an earlier flight," the priest answered, pulling himself up from the chair.

Tim took Conner's offered hand and Conner's felt how cold and weak it was. The priest nudged his head in the direction of the small restaurant off the lobby and said, "Let's get some coffee."

After the thin, blonde waitress brought their coffee, Conner looked at Tim's gray face. As the priest nervously folded and unfolded an empty sugar packet, Conner held no malice in his heart for the priest.

"Father Tim, I'm not angry about what you did. I'm sure you thought it was the right thing to do. I only want to know the truth."

Tim's bloodshot eyes came up to Conner's face. "The truth isn't as simple as that."

"As a priest you know that the truth is always simple. It's only lies that are complicated," Conner replied before taking a sip of his hot coffee. "But I do have one question, Father." The question Conner was about to ask was difficult, but he had to know the answer. "Did Dad know what you were doing?"

The priest's head moved from side to side while his eyes never left Conner's face. "Jack doesn't know a thing about it, and that's the truth."

Tim's answer took a weight off Conner's heart and he nodded with relief.

Then Tim drew in a long breath and threaded his fingers together. He lowered his eyes to his folded hands as if he was about to pray. "Twenty years ago, the day you left Ireland, I got two phone calls. The first was from Gerard O'Connor, the attorney who got that bogus passport so you could get out of Ireland. Gerard said to meet Jack at O'Hara airport. Minutes later, a second call came in. It was from a man who introduced himself as Barra Malone. He said he had something he'd like to trade for a favor."

When Tim's gaze lifted to Conner's face, repentance clung to the downward slant of the priest's eyes. "Do you know anything about Project Children?"

Conner angled his head and narrowed his eyes as he tried to remember if he'd heard that before. "I'm not sure, but the name sounds familiar."

"Project Children is the one that got Catholic and Protestant kids out of Ireland to spend a few weeks together in America."

After a hard sigh, Tim pushed out the rest of his explanation. "What Barra wanted was an exchange. He'd make sure there was an abundance of children in the program from that end in exchange for small pieces of information about you. I knew I was making a deal with the devil, but those children's lives were at stake."

Tim balled his fist until the tension turned his knuckles white, but his gaze remained lowered as he continued. "Barra kept his word. With every child that got into the program, I kept mine."

Then Tim looked directly into Conner's eyes and said, "I know I broke a trust, but I'd do it all again, even if Project Children saved only one life."

He understood where the priest was coming from and what it meant to save a life. If there were more people who cared, not a single child would ever cry himself to sleep because of fear or an empty belly.

Conner reached across the table and pressed his hand atop Tim's aged ones. Hearing the priest's confession made Conner realize that his promise to Di was more than just words. Maybe he had been led back for something larger than just finding himself.

While Conner drew in a slow breath, Peter's words echoed in his head, "Ya'll be knowin' the right path."

Maybe destiny was playing a part in all this. Maybe Di was right. All his life he'd carried the vision of the little girl with the flower. Was that image just a soft memory of Ireland, or was his heart branded with the vision of his destiny? Conner smiled softly at Tim.

Cala had always said there's one true love in our lives, and that name is imprinted on our heart before we're born. She knew that Jack was hers long before he'd made that trip to Ireland.

Di's image floated into Conner's mind. The soft contours of her face and the blue fire in her eyes squeezed his heart. She touched something very deep inside him when she handed him the flower, and when he held her in his arms, he felt complete. Was it only a sweet memory, or was his heart reading the name that was branded on it?

After a few sips of coffee, Conner said, "Well, I'm going to contact Barra to see if I can save one more life. Want to come along, Father Tim?"

Tim smiled and nodded his answer.

Conner slammed the flat of his hands on the table and leaned forward. He pinned Barra with his eyes. "What do I have that you'll trade for?"

Barra cocked his head back and opened his eyes wide. "What's that ya're sayin'?"

"I asked, what have I got that you want?" Conner gave a sharp nod to insure Barra understood. "I'll trade whatever it is, for one life."

"Would ya be walkin' that by me once more?" Confusion made Barra's eyes shift over Conner's face.

Conner stepped away from the table and pulled his spine straight. After he'd pulled each vertebra taut, he said, "I want you to kick Marcus O'Dea's ass out of your group and make sure that he doesn't get into any other 'Irish fraternity.' Now, if there's something I have that you want," Conner added one sharp nod of his head to stress his point, "we have a trade."

With a quick glance at Tim's face, Barra snapped his gaze back to Conner. "So 'tis why ya've brought yar priest then, to be sure the deal is sealed proper like?"

Conner snorted before he said, "Sorry, I thought you two already knew each other." Turning to the priest, Conner said, "Father Tim Sladek, I'd like you to meet Barra Malone."

Barra jerked his head in Tim's direction. With a smile slicing across the man's thin lips, Barra shot his hand out for the priest to shake. "'Tis a grand pleasure to be a meetin' ya at last, Father."

The way the priest kept his hand tucked in his pocket and his jaw locked pleased Conner. Conner nudged his chin in Tim's direction then said to Barra, "You made a trade with him to get what you wanted, so I'm offering you the same deal."

After pulling his handshake back, Barra cornered his eyes down to his empty hand and stared at it for a full minute. Over his curled lips, Barra spat out, "I'm thinkin' there might be somethin' that'll give me the time I wanted to spend with you. I'm thinkin' that ya can take Marcus's place until I get a replacement for the lad."

Widening his eyes to get all of Barra's narrow face in his sights, Conner asked, "What?" He'd stretched out the word in a classic slow motion fashion. "Could you explain yourself since I don't have my Barra dictionary handy?"

Barra's smug smile was back in place, and Conner dug his nails into his palms.

"I said ya take the boy's place."

Conner cocked his head and threw out his words. "You're crazy!"

"Well, ya asked what I wanted." Barra gave an exaggerated shrug and flared out the fingers of both hands in a gesture of finality. "I told ya I want ya to take his place." Withdrawing splayed fingers, he shrugged again but this time only with one shoulder as he continued, "I'm in need of every man I've got. Ya take his place. Marcus can leave. 'Tis a simple deal and the only one I'll be makin'."

Tim pulled himself up to his full length, which brought him up a head taller than both Conner and Barra. The red stain of anger filled the spaces between his freckles while he cut Barra a hard glare through narrowed eyes. "You can't be serious," Tim shouted.

Barra didn't flinch against the priest's assault. The lifelessness in his eyes sent a shiver up Conner's spine. "Oh, but I am, Father. I'm as serious as I was twenty years ago when I made that deal with you."

"You're telling me you've saved your son's life so you can get him killed?" A furious storm flashed in Tim's eyes. "What's the logic in that?"

"The logic is, Niall wants Marcus." Barra turned his piercing glare to Conner. The smug, self-confident smile on Barra's face turned cruel and wicked. Conner wanted to punch his fist into the man's lifeless eyes. Instead, Conner held his temper in check.

"So do we have a deal? I know ya'll be choosin' the right path." Barra's words cut into the silence and thundered in Conner's head.

"The right path isn't that one," Tim spit out, "and you damn well know it."

Tim turned from Barra to Conner. He raked his fingers through his thick red hair. The priest slowly shook his head from side to side as he pleaded with Conner, "You can't consider doing this, Conner."

With fury blazing in his eyes, Tim snapped his gaze to Barra and seethed out, "You're insane. What you're proposing is ludicrous."

The priest was about to say more when Conner interrupted Tim's tirade. "I came here thinking you'd have some compassion for one of your own. I can see there's none in your eyes. Your soul is already dead. Your body is just putting in the time."

Over his curled lip, Barra said, "That's the only deal I have for ya."

The priest looked pleadingly into Conner's eyes. "Please, you mustn't do this."

Conner sighed. "Destiny brought me back here. Now, I have a chance to save one individual, just like all those you saved, Father Tim."

"But I gave those children something better. What you're thinking about doing will put you right back where Jack took you from. You'll be throwing all those years of love he and Cala gave you right down the drain."

"It's the only way I have to save a life," Conner answered with a confirming nod of his head.

With beseeching eyes, Tim pressed his hand to his chest and shook his head. The reply Conner gave was a slow nod to Barra.

Conner clearly understood he was making a deal with the devil and that what Tim had said was right. Yet, this was the only way Conner could fulfill his promise. He'd give Marcus a life and along with it Conner would save Di and her family grief. In exchange he'd be in Barra's employ for a few weeks. Conner nodded once more but this time it wasn't for Barra, it was to confirm in Conner's mind this was the right path.

Barra stared at the floor while the others stared at him. "I've won," he said, more to himself than out loud. "The boy is mine now."

"Ya confuse me, Barra. Ya've saved yar son's life and then ya're willin' to end it?" Mickey's voice drew Barra's gaze up from the pockmarked concrete floor.

"Ya're not realizin' that 'tis the cause that's the important matter. It makes no never mind about the individual, be it son or father."

"But he's yar own flesh and blood," Mickey said through curled lips.

Barra slowly lowered to the crate. He kept his eyes locked on Mickey's face while Barra pressed a balled fist to the middle of his stomach. He willed the pain to stop. When it eased, with a voice that was heavy with pain, Barra said, "I'd be sacrificin' me own blood and any others. Bein' me son doesn't make him any better than the rest of ya."

Mick turned and walked away saying, "Ya've got Satan in yar soul, 'tis the truth of it."

"I've neither got Satan nor God. I'm a patriot," Barra called to Mickey's back.

Without turning to Barra, Mickey laughed out, "Ya're a madman, that's what ya are."

Chapter 22

"He said *what*?"

Cala did a slow turn from the sink to the stove as she answered her husband's demanding question. "Conner said he's got to save the life of a boy named Marcus O'Dea. So he'll be staying in Ireland for a few more weeks."

With her back pressed to the stove, she strangled the dishtowel she held with both hands. Cala knew she needed strength to say the rest. "Tim said Conner's real father had hired Conner to work for Ireland."

"Work for Ireland?" Jack said with narrowed eyes. "What the hell does that mean?"

Cala sighed. "What it means is, no good. They call themselves patriots, but what they are, are nothing more than murderers."

Jack's back was stiff as he sat at the table. The veins in his neck bulged with anger well before he slammed his fist on the wooden surface. "What in the hell is the kid thinking? And who in the hell is this Marcus O'Dea?"

She slid into the chair across from her husband and kept her gaze pinned on his face. Once she had laid her hand over her husband's fist, she answered, "You met the lad when he was a wee babe the night of Samhain."

Without a word Jack pulled his hands from under hers and jumped out of his chair. He was on his way out of the kitchen when Cala shouted to his back, "Where are you going?"

"To Tirnageata to talk some sense into our son," Jack called out over his shoulder.

Cala sprung onto her feet and raced after her husband. "Wait up for me."

"Who the bloody hell gave ya permission to be talkin' to Barra about me?" Marcus asked as he jerked Conner around by the back of his sweater. "And just who told yar parents to come to Ireland to be tellin' me Mam and Da what I'm doin' these days?" Marcus' bellowing voice drew up the heads of the guests that milled around the hotel lobby.

Glaring hard into Marcus's angry eyes, Conner said through the line of his sneering lips, "I told you once before, you touch me and you'll never use that hand." Conner shook out of Marcus's grip, then added, "For your information my parents are in Chicago, so no one told your parents jack shit."

"Well, there was a couple that's doin' a good impression of Jack and Cala Wolfe at me parent's this minute," Marcus spit out.

Conner slashed his eyes over Marcus's face searching for the truth. "Are you shittin' me?" Conner saw no lies in the young man's eyes. "What in the hell is going on?"

"I don't give a fiddler's fart what's goin' on. Ya've no right to interfere."

"You might be some goddamn genius, but you don't know your ass from a hole in the ground. Your sister asked me to do something to save you. To be honest, I don't give a rat's ass what happens to you, but I don't want to see your mother crying at the side of your grave when I can stop that from happening."

Marcus pulled his shoulders back and slowly shook his head from side to side. Then he matched Conner shout for shout. "Nothin's gonna happen to me."

"I know you believe you've got some inside track, being an Indigo and all, but as far as I'm concerned you're still a prick with his head up his ass." Conner huffed out a breath through the sliced opening of his mouth. "I'll give you ten to one you'll end up being a statistic like all the other misguided patriots." Conner spit the word "patriot" out as if it was rotten in his mouth. "Instead of turning my back, I'm going to make sure your mother," Conner sighed hard, "and your sister know I did all I could. If I can't stop you, then I'll take it one step further. I'm going to make sure they both know you didn't give two shits about them." His anger-spiked words shortened his lungs and Conner drew in a long breath to refill them.

"Ya got it all wrong," Marcus interrupted. "'Tis because of them that I'm doin' what I'm doin."

"Don't even try to shovel that bullshit in my direction. You're the one that's got it wrong and that brain of yours can't comprehend you're fighting for a cause that is going to kill not only you, but also everyone that cares about you. If you weren't so wrapped up in your own ego you'd see what you're doing. So get your sorry ass out of here and be grateful that you've got people that love you."

"You've got that too, Niall," Jack's voice came from behind Conner. When Conner turned, there stood not only his parents, but also Ellen and Tom.

"Dad, Mom, what the hell are you doing here?"

"We're here to talk just as much sense into you as you're trying to do with Marcus," Jack answered. "Are you willing to listen or will you break your mother's heart just to keep your word?"

Conner knew his dad had just played his trump card, so he offered Jack a soft smile. "Dad, you risked your life to save mine. Is that any different than what I'm doing?"

"It sure as hell is different. You were a kid. Marcus is nearly a man."

"You said that right, he's 'nearly' a man." Conner looked into Jack's face and saw the same pain, sorrow, and love that he'd seen in Jack's eyes the night he rescued Conner from the Irish police. It tore at Conner's heart, but he knew this was the right path.

"Dad, I know I can save him and I'm going to do that. All I have to do is give Barra one week to find a replacement for Marcus."

"Then ya'll be takin' me place is it?" Marcus broke in with his question. The arrogant smile on his face matched the look in his eyes.

Conner slashed his gaze at the younger man before he answered, "Yes."

With a half-cocked smile and one raised eyebrow, Marcus asked, "Then ya'll be the one distractin' the *garda* in Omagh today?"

Ellen stepped forward. Terror darted from her eyes as her hand flayed over her heart. "Omagh?" she asked the one-word question in nearly a whisper.

Marcus sliced his gaze at his mother. "Aye, 'tis where Barra wanted the next callin' card be placed today."

"OH SWEET JESUS!" Ellen screamed. "That's where Di went to buy supplies for the kids at the center."

With both her hands strangling Conner's arm, Ellen shouted, "OH LORD, NIALL! You must stop them please, please. Oh God, please! Please bring me daughter home," Ellen cried out through her tears.

Tom raced out the hotel door with Ellen's screams following after him. He was in the driver's seat of his truck with the motor already fired up when Jack climbed into the passenger's side. Both Conner and Marcus leapt onto the bed of the truck as it pulled away from the curb.

The way the small vehicle bounced over the country roads was clear indication nothing was going to slow Tom down. When the truck reached the pavement, though the ride had become smooth, Conner was still shaking. He knew it had nothing to do with the condition of the roads.

They'd been traveling just over an hour when Tom honked the horn and shouted out the opened window, "Omagh!"

Because Conner sat with his back pressed to the cab of the truck, he couldn't get a clear view of the town. Considering the speed at which the truck was traveling, he wouldn't dare chance standing up.

Suddenly, an enormous blast rocked the truck. The percussion knocked the air out of Conner's lungs. He choked and sucked in a breath as Tom pulled the vehicle to a skidding stop. Conner and Marcus quickly leapt to their feet and looked out over the top of the truck.

Rising up against the azure sky was a huge black cloud. As it clawed its way up to the heavens, Conner's blood went cold. He dug his nails into the metal as a wave of nausea washed over him. Death impregnated the cloud and shrouded the earth with a deafening silence. Desolation poured into his soul and Conner's heart screamed with the pain.

SHE WAS DEAD!

Chapter 23

The vehicle lurched forward, and Conner held on tightly until the truck came to another chattered stop. When it did, Conner's mind splintered at the unbelievable scene that stretched out before him. The devastation held Conner in complete disbelief.

Market Street's narrow width was blanketed with splintered wood and chunks of plaster from the row of shattered buildings. A single wooden door, its top braced against a lamppost, stood askew atop a mound of debris. Monstrous gaping holes had been torn out of the roofs as if an angry giant had grabbed handfuls of the building and tossed them into the street. The huge plate glass window of a shop had been blown out, yet the display was perfectly intact.

Tattered curtains flapped through glassless window frames on the buildings' upper floors. The fabric excitedly waved in the wind as if trying to surrender to an enemy. To whom does a building surrender? Terrorists don't give a damn about flesh and bone, why would they care about something made of bricks and wood?

In the distance a siren wailed, as one after another heart-wrenching screams came out from the rubble. The cacophony of sounds and devastation conjured images of Hell. Yes, this was Hell, one that only man could make.

Together Conner and Marcus jumped out of the truck's bed and raced after Tom and Jack. As the older O'Dea ran, he pointed his finger at a building with no face and shouted, "Start at Kells."

Without the slightest hesitation, the four leapt over mounds of rubble and rivers of broken glass to the most demolished building on the street. Marcus rushed ahead of the others. He ran as if he knew exactly where to go. Conner kept on the young man's heels. With each step Conner's heart whispered the name that had been branded there before time began. *"Daligherat, Daligherat, Daligherat."* When there was no answer, Conner's heart knew there never would be again.

Suddenly, Marcus stopped and fell to his knees. Frantically, he clawed through a mound of the shattered building. "She's here. I've found her," he screamed.

The others ran to his side and wildly dug through the pile with him. As Conner ripped away a large piece of broken plaster, Di's pale face and unseeing eyes looked up at him. He sucked in a ragged breath and closed his eyes. Death had struck again. This time it took a part of him. It took his heart.

After guiding, his daughter's head into his lap, Tom gently brushed away the dirt that clung to her face. His tears splashed down onto Di's cheeks while he rocked her with his sobs.

"Get her out of here. NOW!" Marcus commanded. "We have to take her to Mam."

Tom ignored his son's demand, but Jack and Conner followed the younger O'Dea's orders. After they pulled the balance of the rubble off the body, Marcus lifted Di into his arms and raced to the truck.

Conner ran ahead and jumped up into the truck's bed. Squatting down on his haunches, he stretched out his arms. "Please, give her to me." Marcus hesitated, but then the young man tenderly placed his sister's lifeless body into Conner's arms.

Cala stood at the open doorway of the cottage while Ellen ran down the stone steps to the truck. Her grief poured out as she repeatedly called out her daughter's name. Tom was out of the truck and wrapping his wife in his arms to share her pain.

Marcus stood at the tailgate with his arms outstretched in a silent petition, but Conner pulled Di's body tighter to him. He wouldn't give her up, not to Marcus, not to death.

"Give her to him, son," Jack said softly.

Conner looked down into Di's face as he mechanically did as his father instructed.

With Di draped across his arms, Marcus turned to his mother. With tears streaming down his face, he choked out, "'Tis sorry I am, Mam. 'Twas me fault."

Ellen cupped Di's chin in her palm and kissed her daughter's death-cloaked face. She murmured soft words to her child.

Cala trembled and looked up to the heavens as her own tears poured down her face. A golden finger of light reached down from the sky and touched just over the hills. Cala's eyes widened, and she quickly came to her friend's side and whispered into Ellen's ear.

Ellen's head flew up. She struck Cala with wide eyes. "Is it possible?"

Slowly, Cala nodded. "We can do it together, but 'tis help we'll need."

"All here will help," Ellen answered with a confirmed absolute.

"But 'tis the strongest one we'll be needin'," Cala said with a raised eyebrow.

After a quick glance to her son, Ellen said, "Marcus knows where to find such a one."

Turning a questioning look to Marcus, Cala sighed. "Only the purest of heart will be doin' us any good."

Without lifting his eyes from his sister's pale face, Marcus answered, "I know just the one that will be meetin' our needs."

While the flames of the four candles flickered against the dying daylight sky, night clouds anxiously gathered along the horizon. Slowly, long shadows stretched into the center of the massive stone circle.

Tim's gaze scanned the breadth of the encompassing megaliths. Time had worn away their bulk, but a power still resonated from these granite monsters. He looked around as he chastised himself. How could he condone such blasphemy by standing within this pagan circle? As his gaze moved from stone to stone, Tim felt a strange charge in the air. The Catholic Church had a stronghold in Ireland, but the way these people worshiped the ancient ways didn't set right with him. The hairs on the back of his neck lifted, and he quickly ran his hand over his prickled skin. He shivered. Even his own skin felt strange to his touch, but then everything about the last few hours had been insurmountably surreal.

Jack leaned to the priest and said just above a whisper, "There's things I've never shared with you about that night twenty years ago, and how it changed the course I was on."

His friend's statement quickly drew Tim's attention. He turned and watched how tiny glints of amber flames flickered in Jack's eyes while ebony shadows deepened the grooves that lined Jack's brow. Tim's heart vibrated.

"You knew that when I left Chicago I was depressed over my son's death," Jack said without the slightest shift in his eyes.

"What you didn't know was that I had decided Ireland was where I'd end my life."

Tim answered, "At the time I wasn't sure, but in my heart I felt that was a possibility. Yet, all I could do was pray I was wrong."

As if he still carried the shame of it, Jack dropped his gaze to the ground then slowly lifted his eyes to the priest's face. "There's a secret my family has kept for hundreds of years." Jack hesitated before saying, "Tirnageata translated means 'the gate.'"

Tim nodded again. "Yes, I know a little Gaelic."

Jack shifted his gaze to the stone altar and added, "The gate is to the dark plain."

Tim turned his full face to Jack. "I don't understand. Isn't the dark plain the name the Celts used for the other world? The world of the dead?"

"Yes," Jack nodded, "the world of the dead. Tirnageata is the gate to that world. Centuries ago, my family was given the gift of being able to open that gate during the Samhain. On that night, loved ones from both plains share one hour together."

Even after Tim took a complete step back from Jack, Jack refused to take his eyes off his wife and Ellen as they prepared Di's body. "That night, on this very spot, I held my infant son in my arms. I smelled his sweetness and heard him call me Daddy."

"You're telling me that you held a child who had died six months earlier?" Tim shook his head and narrowed his eyes. "Did they hypnotize you or something?"

Jack softly smiled and said, "I'm telling you this so that you'll keep an open mind and be prepared to witness the miracle of what love can do."

Before Tim could digest what Jack had just told him, Robert Jameson stepped up to the two men with an extended hand and introduced himself. "I'm Robert, a student at the center where Di works."

Jack immediately took the boy's offered hand. After shaking Jack's hand, Robert offered his hand to Tim. When Tim shook it, electricity rippled up the priest's arm. Robert looked deep into Tim's eyes and said, "The Celtic law of responsibility is as ancient as time."

Tim looked down the length of his nose at the youth. "What?"

Robert pulled back his hand and answered, "If you harm someone in anyway, restitution must be made."

With a twisted face, Tim asked, "Are you saying that this happened to Di because she harmed someone?" Shaking his head, Tim added, "I can't believe that."

Stabbing his eyes straight into Tim's, Robert answered, "I didn't say Di did." The teen moved away without looking back at the two men.

As the priest watched Robert walk to Marcus's side, his chest tightened. He pressed his hand to his heart. Was it the weight of the sin he carried that Robert was talking about?

The priest shifted his gaze to Di's father. Tom's tall, lean frame stood half in the shadow and half in the light. His eyes were locked on his daughter's body while he tapped out a slow steady beat on the skin drum he held curled in his arm.

Tim's heart fluttered as if to come in cadence with the steady rhythm of the drum. Still, the change in beat didn't ease the heaviness that collected in Tim's heart.

Chapter 24

The last time Conner had been inside the circle of megalith giants, they had vibrated with music and laughter. It was the night the people of Tirnageata celebrated Samhain. It's believed that this ancient ritual is the forerunner to Halloween, but this pagan holiday was really far more than that to these villagers. Their celebration was in the tradition of their ancestors, with a great respect for both life and death. That long-ago night, Conner remembered how the monster stones seemed pleased that this village would share that night with them. It was that same night a beautiful little girl gave him a flower. Conner leaned on that memory for twenty years. He dug his nails into his palms and squeezed his eyes tight. When he'd at last found that girl, instead of holding her close, he walked away from the one he needed the most. Her love.

Conner stretched his gaze up to the largest giant. Clearly, this king of the stones guarded a secret. What was it? Was it its knowledge of the past, or of the future? Conner tried to listen to the whispering wind, but the reverberating anguish in his heart refused to allow any thought into his head but grief.

He lowered his gaze to Di's face. The granite altar that her body laid on was smooth. Lights from the candles illuminated his reflected image in the glass like sheen. They were together. The way they should have been in life. Now half of her soul was dead. The half that held love.

Conner drew a finger over the line of Di's cold lips.
The memory of that sweet five-year-old girl's smile and of the flower she had handed him had always softened the hard

memories of his last days in Ireland. That memory of the little girl had given him the courage to face life, but the woman's smile had given his heart the hope to love.

He breathed in a ragged breath and brushed a strand of hair from her forehead. Death now held that smile captive, and he'd never see it again. The thought tightened his throat. Gently, he ran his knuckles down the soft contours of her death-washed face. Once again, he was left behind, but this time it was more than loneliness that emptied his heart. His soul would be sentenced to a purgatory without her. He fell to his knees and buried his tears into her chest.

As Tim and Jack stood in the background, the O'Dea men cocooned Ellen between them. Cala turned to Ellen and questioned, "Are you sure you want to be the soul to exchange places with her?"

"Yes," Ellen answered, "I'm the one that must."

Tom snapped out, "Ya've no right to be the one. I am her father. I'm the one responsible for keepin' her safe."

Ellen turned her tear-streaked face up to her husband. "But 'twas I that carried her inside me. I gave her life the first time. 'Tis me should be doin' it again."

Marcus cut his mother's words off with a loud, "NO! 'Tis me fault she's dead." He slashed his red eyes to Cala and begged, "Ya must be replacin' her soul with mine."

Conner strongly shook his head from side to side. He stepped forward and looked directly into Cala's face. "If the exchange is possible it can't be either of them. That would only bring Daligherat grief." Looking down into Di's face, Conner added, "If anyone is to do this, it must be me."

Jack snapped to attention and quickly took one long step to his son's side. He locked his fingers around Conner's shoulders and jerked his son's attention around to him. "Are you crazy? You can't do that, son."

Cala's eyes flashed with horror as her hand came up to her mouth to mute the scream that tried to squeeze through her fingers.

"Yes, I can, Dad." Conner stepped back out of Jack's grip. The young man's emotions glazed his eyes. Conner's voice cracked, making him clear his throat before he said, "All my life, death refused to take me when others around me fell. I finally understand why death continued to elude me. I was being saved,

saved for this."

Conner looked down into Di's face. "She'd said I was her destiny." He stroked her hand. "She said she had prayed for help and I was sent. So, I must be the one to take her place in the dark plain."

Tim shifted from side to side and his chest tightened at what he'd heard. He dug his nails into his palms as he fought to keep his mouth shut. There was no way God was going to allow this foolishness. His souls are His for all eternity. Why would these people even be arguing over something as ridiculous as a soul exchange?

Turning his eyes to Jack's, Conner sighed. "Dad, you have to understand that this *is* my destiny, the destiny that you saved me for."

Conner then turned to Cala and added, "This is the path that had been set before I took my first breath. This is my contract."

Jack speared Cala with his eyes. "He's going to give his life. Do you hear him?" The rough lines of Jack's face softened. The igniting anger in his dark eyes turned to embers as he added, "Please, for the love of God, talk to him. Tell the boy what he is going to do is wrong."

Wringing her hands, Cala answered, "How can I tell him 'tis wrong when we both know the part destiny played in our lives? We must walk the path we've chosen."

"Stop that," Jack lashed out. "You're talking like you agree with his decision. Twenty years ago you screamed at me not to even consider doing something as foolish as taking my life, yet you're condoning our son's decision to give up his?"

Cala shook with tears. "Yours was a selfish act, born from the grief you carried, but our son is givin' a gift for the one he loves."

With a strong shake of his head, Jack corrected, "Yes, but not his life."

Conner searched Jack's face as he spoke, "Dad, you gave me life for a purpose. That purpose is Daligherat's life."

Jack's shoulders fell forward and his head came down with them. Conner moved to his parents and wrapped them in his arms. When he released them, he stepped back to Di's body and placed a kiss on her cold lips. He turned, and it was then that Tim saw total contentment in the young man's eyes. The priest's mind spun. Suddenly, prayers were tumbling out Tim's mouth. Praying harder than he'd ever done in his life, Tim's lungs shortened, and the ache strangled his heart.

"Let this fluid from the Adler tree cleanse this woman," Cala and Ellen chanted as they washed Di's body with a brown stained liquid.

Taking Di's face in her hands, Ellen gently ran the brown stained cloth over her daughter's forehead and eyelids while Cala cleansed Di's legs and arms. Once the body was washed, they draped it in a pale yellow robe. Cala squeezed a red mistletoe berry over Di's lips. Ellen followed right behind her with a white berry.

As the juice ran down Di's chin, their echoed chant now changed to a more demanding tone. "Hoof and horn, hoof and horn, all that dies shall be reborn. Corn and grain, corn and grain, all that falls shall rise again." Each spoken word matched the beats of Tom's skin drum.

With hands raised and joined, Robert and Marcus called out to the gray night sky. "We call to the greeter at the gates of death and life. Be with us. Join our rite. Blessed be."

Conner watched as the dark clouds churned in the sky, rolling and folding onto one another, erasing even the tiniest of stars. The black void siphoned his mind into the dark abyss of complete and utter loneliness. Beads of sweat followed his spine.

Tim's chest grew even tighter with each prayer he said. He clutched the crucifix that hung around his neck in his hand, digging the sharp corners into his palm.

"Oh My God" Tim said as he looked at Di's prostrated body, "save us from the fires of hell, take my soul to heaven. Cleanse me, strengthen me, heal me. Sweet Heart of Mary, be my salvation."

Each word of Tim's prayer took its turn with Ellen's and Cala's mantra while Robert and Marcus squeezed their words into the empty spaces. The blend of dissonant voices with the beats of the drum took on the quality of a Gregorian chant.

When Tim looked up at the pitch-black sky, a semi-circle of twelve stars arched overhead. With his eyes locked onto the apparition, he repeatedly struck his breast with his crucifix-enclosed hand. "Take my soul to heaven, Blessed Mother. Take my soul to your Son, so I may beg Him forgiveness for the sin I committed against a friend."

The stars enlarged and spread a fanning light down into the circle of megaliths. Everyone froze, mesmerized by the bright light that cut a downward slash from the heavens to the ground. Suddenly, out from the arch walked a blonde-haired teenage boy.

"Peter," Conner called out, taking a small step forward.

Without saying a word, Peter smiled at his brother then moved to the altar and placed his hand on Di's forehead. He leaned to her ear and whispered.

Di's eyes fluttered open, but the disorientation in them marked her confusion. Conner instantly stepped to her side and lifted her hand to his lips. She smiled at him and slowly sat up. Conner released a long hard sigh and wrapped her in his arms.

From the outer edge of the circle, Tim heard the soft words of thanks that Conner spoke with each kiss he placed on Di's face. The miracle he'd just witnessed could have come only from God. The ache in Tim's heart strangled the air in his lungs. Clutching his chest, Tim silently collapsed to the ground.

Conner turned to Peter and said, "I know the right path. I'm ready to follow it now."

Peter didn't answer. Instead, he walked back into the light. When he reached the crest, Peter turned and extended one hand to the group.

After a hard sigh, Conner kissed Di's forehead and unwound her from his arms. He took a single step and suddenly stopped. Inside the fanning light, two silhouettes walked deeper into the yellow center, fading more with each step.

"Tim!" Jack shouted and ran to his friend's side, but the darkness around Tim's mouth answered Jack's unasked question.

Cala jerked around to where Tim had stood. She hesitated, and then raced to his side. Tears clogged her throat as she repeatedly called out the priest's name.

Jack curled his arm around Cala's shoulder as they wept together.

"The restitution has been made," Robert said to the wide light as it shrunk to a small orb.

Conner helped Di off the altar and into her mother's opened arms. He quickly went to Tim's body and knelt down at the priest's side. Conner had no control over the tears that fell with his words. "Thank you for your gift, my dear friend."

Epilogue

September 20, 2006

Conner stood with his back to the window and watched the early morning sunlight tenderly touch Di's sleep-softened face. In seven years, much had changed in his life. Barra died six months after the Omagh bombing. Mickey told Conner that the group had disbanded. However, he was sure most of the men had been absorbed into other factions, but not Marcus. He'd gone back to the university and gotten his medical degree.

As the sunlight shimmered through Di's hair, Conner smiled. The long strands that fanned out over the white pillow and cascaded over her alabaster shoulders excited him, and his lips tingled with the memory of kissing her soft skin.

He sighed and turned to the window. Ireland hadn't welcomed him back after twenty years, but now it opened its arms to him. He'd come back in search of answers. What it gave him was his destiny.

"We've a few more hours before we need be up, husband mine. Would ya be likin' to share them in bed?"

Di's sleep-soaked voice warmed Conner's body. He turned with a smile already spreading across his face. "If I do, we'll be late for the meeting."

"'Tis understandin' they'll be since ya're the one that'll be runnin' the show."

After sliding into bed, he pulled Di's back to his chest. The warmth of her body seeped through him, and he brushed a kiss on her cheek. "It's the church that really handles things. I'm just in charge of finding the children."

Di turned in his arms and cut him a hard glare that ignited the fire in her eyes. "Ya've been able to be a savin' so many with one project or another. Ya've gotten the church to open its purse strings for the homeless shelters. And just who was it now that got those American companies to fund Robert's research study about the DNA changes in Indigo children?"

Conner tightened his arms around her. "If I can save one child, I'm happy."

"'Tis time for Gran to arrive yet?" The three high-pitched voices that easily cut through the wooden door had Conner struggling to keep his laughter silent.

"No need for ya to be tryin' to keep them from knowin' ya're up. Those three children of yars can't be fooled, ya know," Di said, adding a jab to Conner's ribs as confirmation.

Sucking in a quick breath to refill the air Di's elbow took away, Conner answered, "Yes, Gran will be here in about an hour."

That was all the invitation the three children needed to bound into the room at neck-breaking speed right into the center of the bed. They chattered away at their parents and each other until the room pulsated with the most pleasant sounds any father could hear. Happy children.

When both the children and the sounds settled down, Conner looked at his six-year-old daughter's cherub face and smiled. The tiny lines that grooved her brow caught his attention. "What's troublin' you, Marissa?"

She rolled onto her side and slowly drew her small finger down the thin scar on Conner's cheek. "'Tis thinkin' I was about the cold winter."

"Rowen. Liam," Di said with a feigned stern look as she gently placed her hand between the twin four-year-old sons to stop them from tickling each other. Without taking her attention off the boys, Di added, "'Tis only September. Are ya anxious to be skatin' and sleddin' then?"

"Not in the least," Marissa answered. "'Twas rememberin' when the boys drowned in Gran's lake, I was."

Conner's gaze slashed from his daughter's face to his wife's, and back again. Taking in a quick breath, Conner asked, "What do you mean, kiddo?"

"Well, Rowen and Liam drowned when they were just four, and Mam and I were the only ones left. I remember how cold it was and how little food we'd had that winter."

"That's not a good dream for a sweet little girl to have, now is it?" Conner asked, smoothing out the lines in her brow with his finger.

Rolling onto her back, she pillowed her hands under her head and corrected, "'Twasn't a dream, Da. Ask Uncle Marcus."

Conner snapped his gaze to Di but she only shrugged her shoulders and skittered out of bed with the three children on her heels. In a blink, Conner was right behind her. He grabbed her around the waist and whispered, "That's from your side of the family."

Di winked and blew him a kiss as she ushered the children out the bedroom door.

About the Author

Living in the Midwest with her family, Sloan considers herself to be an extremely lucky woman. She'll tell you that not only has she managed to have her dreams, but she's living them as well.

With her first book, "The Dark Plain", Sloan's innovative writing style took the publishing world by storm winning numerous prestigious awards. This captivating story now continues with "The Dark Shield". Reviewers are claiming that once again Sloan St.James has brought a fresh and unique story that tugs at the reader's heartstrings.

Other Books by Sloan St. James

The Dark Plain
Tiger Publications

Sin stained his soul, but her love blocked his journey into Hell.

After the death of his son single dad, Jack Wolfe returns to his ancestral home in Ireland. There he meets Cala McCoy. Their instant attraction confuses him. Yet, Cala knows their love has transcended time. She also knows that she must replace the guilt and grief in Jack's heart with forgiveness. Only an ancient Druid ritual of lifting the veil between the plain of the living and dead can save him. But will dark forces stop her and sentence the soul mates to another 800 years apart

Coming soon:

The Dark Legacy
Tiger Publications

Though life has many uncertain outcomes, death is a constant, or is it?

In 800 AD Ireland's religious beliefs was a blend called Celtic Christianity. They embraced Catholicism only after it was stirred though Paganism. It was a slow process for many to change their lives. However, for Bronach Deisi her life changed with the slash of a Viking's sword. Though she managed to cheat death, the reaper of souls refused to be denied. It extracted its debit from those she loves. One by one they were taken from her. In her pain she turns to God for help. His answer comes wrapped in the cloak of a Druid. Though their association is strained, time tempers it into one that leaves its mark on generations of Clan Donegal.